James pointed to Olivia's clothes. "At first I thought you were the lady who tried to sell me life insurance last week."

"So I'm wearing nice clothes," Olivia said huffily. "What's the big deal?"

"No big deal. I just thought it was some kind of joke, that's all."

"I'm not trying to make a joke," she informed him. "If you want to know the truth, the way I *used* to dress was a joke."

"The way you used to dress was th⸱⸱⸱ ⸱h, Olivia."

"Oh, come on⸱ ⸱⸱⸱⸱⸱ ⸱⸱⸱⸱⸱⸱ ⸱ just an act. I d⸱⸱⸱⸱⸱

"Why? Are y⸱⸱⸱ joined the world ⸱⸱⸱⸱ That you don't n⸱⸱⸱⸱⸱

"Well, now that ⸱⸱⸱ mention it, I guess I have," Olivia said.

James stared at her silently for a moment. Finally, he spoke. "I can't believe you just said that. Are you the same person who agreed that painting is something you *have* to do, something that's part of who you are?"

"That was before," Olivia said irritably as she began to pace. She could feel James's eyes on her, and she prickled with indignation and confusion. He was making her say things she didn't really mean! He was making her sound cold and materialistic. He was making her defend positions she suddenly wasn't really sure she wanted to defend!

Bantam Books in the Sweet Valley High series
Ask your bookseller for the books you have missed

SWEET VALLEY HIGH

Super Star

OLIVIA'S STORY

Written by
Kate William

Created by
FRANCINE PASCAL

BANTAM BOOKS

NEW YORK • TORONTO • LONDON • SYDNEY • AUCKLAND

RL 6, age 12 and up

OLIVIA'S STORY
A Bantam Book / December 1991

Sweet Valley High is a registered trademark of Francine Pascal

Conceived by Francine Pascal

Produced by Daniel Weiss Associates, Inc.
33 West 17th Street
New York, NY 10011

Cover art by James Mathewuse

ISBN 0-553-29359-1

Published simultaneously in the United States and Canada

Bantam Books are published by Bantam Books, a division of Bantam Doubleday
Dell Publishing Group, Inc. Its trademark, consisting of the words "Bantam
Books" and the portrayal of a rooster, is Registered in U.S. Patent and Trademark
Office and in other countries. Marca Registrada. Bantam Books, 666 Fifth Avenue,
New York, New York 10103.

PRINTED IN THE UNITED STATES OF AMERICA

OPM   0 9 8 7 6 5 4 3 2 1

OLIVIA'S
STORY

One

Elizabeth Wakefield hitched her backpack up on her shoulder, opened the door, and walked into Sweet Valley High's newspaper office.

"Liz!" cried a frantic voice. "How do you spell *grotesque*?"

Laughing, Elizabeth put her books down. "Olivia, *what* are you describing now? Some poor freshman's attempt in Advertising Design class?"

"Ha ha," Olivia Davidson said with an impish smile. "I'm writing a review of that new science fiction movie, for your information." She stuck her pencil behind her ear and began paging through a dog-eared dictionary.

As arts editor of *The Oracle*, it was Olivia's job to cover movies, school concerts, student art shows, and TV specials. The fact that all she really wanted to do was paint never prevented her from doing an excellent job for the school paper.

Elizabeth pulled up a chair next to her friend. "Did you really sit through the whole movie?" she asked with an exaggerated shudder. "I can't even bear to watch the advertisements for it on television. That part where the aliens take their skin off and—yuck. It's completely revolting."

"Well, I confess that I did watch most of it like this," Olivia said, putting both hands in front of her eyes and peeking between her fingers. "But I saw enough to know that every guy in this school will probably love it and cheer like a maniac during all of the most disgusting scenes."

"Any exploding body parts?" Elizabeth asked lightly.

"Tons," Olivia replied.

Elizabeth nodded. "Todd will love it," she said.

"Yeah, sure!" Olivia laughed. "Your boyfriend is probably the only guy I know who *wouldn't* love it."

Elizabeth grinned, and pulled her sun-streaked blond hair back into a ponytail. "Did you do anything really fun over Thanksgiving, or were you obliged to watch more horrible movies in the line of duty?"

"I went to the museum in L.A.," her friend said with a sudden, vibrant smile.

Elizabeth knew that by "the museum in L.A." Olivia meant the Museum of Contemporary Art. Whenever she had the time and money, Olivia took a day trip to Los Angeles to see what was happening in the art world. She always returned from those visits electrified with ideas and enthusiasm.

Elizabeth smiled at Olivia's obvious excitement. "Did you see anything good?" she asked.

"Well, since you asked . . ." Olivia began mischievously. "I saw a show of Abstract Expressionists that was just *incredible*."

"What *is* abstract expressionism? I'm not really sure what that term means," Elizabeth admitted.

Olivia dragged her hand through her wild, curly mop of brown hair. Elizabeth noticed a blue paint stain on the inside of Olivia's wrist.

"There's nothing figurative about abstract expressionism," Olivia explained. "The pictures are total emotional expression."

Elizabeth nodded slowly. "You mean, the artists don't paint pictures of real things."

"Emotions *are* real things," Olivia said earnestly. "Joy, greed, fear—"

"OK, OK!" Elizabeth cut in, laughing. "I think I know what you mean."

Olivia grinned. "But you still like pictures of *things* better, right?"

3

"Does that make me hopelessly dull and unartistic?" Elizabeth asked ruefully.

"Hopelessly," Olivia teased.

Elizabeth picked up a pencil and bounced the eraser lightly on her palm. Although she did not share Olivia's excitement about contemporary art, she really did admire her friend's dedication to her own painting. To Elizabeth's mind, Olivia was one of a kind. Her style of dressing, how she spent her free time, the things she considered important—everything about Olivia was proof of how deeply she felt about art. Sometimes Elizabeth felt that compared to Olivia, most of the other students at Sweet Valley High seemed frivolous and empty-headed, the type of people who always ran with the pack. Olivia seemed unaware that there even was a pack. She was out there on her own.

"So, what do you think you'll be doing over the winter vacation?" Elizabeth asked, resting her chin on her palm.

"Winter vacation?" Olivia rolled her eyes. "That's almost a month away. I *never* plan that far ahead, Liz. I just can't do it."

Elizabeth's blue-green eyes sparkled. "Now you sound just like my sister."

For a moment, Olivia was speechless. Elizabeth realized that to be compared to her own twin sister, Jessica, must have been something of a shock to Olivia. After all, Jessica's main interests were boys, cheerleading, the Pi Beta Alpha sorority, and going to the beach. Her notorious inability to plan ahead, unless there was a cute boy involved, was the only similarity there could ever be between Jessica Wakefield and Olivia Davidson.

Olivia opened her mouth to respond, and then turned pink.

"I'm sorry." Elizabeth laughed. "You don't have to find a polite way to say you don't like being compared to Jessica."

Olivia let her breath out in a rush. "Thanks," she said as she brushed her hair back again.

"Did you know that you have blue paint on your wrist?" Elizabeth asked her.

"Oh. That must be from last night. I'm taking an oil painting class at the Forester Art School."

"Really? That's great!" Elizabeth said. "I've heard they're very selective about who they accept."

Olivia shrugged, but her flushed face showed how thrilled she really was. "Oh, I guess I just meet their incredibly high standards," she said.

"I think that's wonderful, Olivia," Elizabeth said warmly. "What kind of paintings are you doing?"

Olivia arched her eyebrows. "Guess."

"Abstract expressionist?" Elizabeth hazarded.

"You got it. The teacher is really great. He doesn't say very much, but he asks tough questions about the work you're doing." Olivia leaned back in her chair and folded her arms. "He makes you think about why you made certain decisions about color or line or shape and if you're wishy-washy about your answer, he lets you know. I love it."

Elizabeth smiled. Maybe she didn't understand abstract expressionism, but she did understand Olivia's enthusiasm. Olivia felt the same way about painting as Elizabeth felt about writing. Elizabeth hoped that one day she would be a successful writer. And she was sure that Olivia could become an accomplished painter if she wanted to.

"Could I see some of your paintings sometime?" Elizabeth asked.

Olivia smiled brightly. "Do you really want to?" she asked.

"I really do. I probably won't *understand* them—"

"I'll tell you how and why I painted each one," Olivia broke in eagerly. "I think knowing the artist's methods and intention really helps to understand a picture."

Elizabeth smiled. "Then it's a deal."

"Listen, I'll give you a crash course right now," Olivia said. "I bet you like the Impressionists' paintings, right? Monet's water lilies, for example?"

"Exactly," Elizabeth admitted.

Olivia nodded. "OK, great. You know how dreamy those pictures are, right? They're nothing like photographs, but you can still identify the water lilies as water lilies. Now take someone like van Gogh and his paintings of sunflowers. van Gogh's methods are very different from Monet's. He uses wild swirls of paint and strange, surprising colors so that the sunflowers express his own mood, his emotions. With expressionism, even more of the artist gets into the image. The painting gets farther away from an exact depiction of an object and deeper into the emotion the artist feels in relation to that object. Finally, the object disappears and only the artist's emotional experience of the object remains."

Elizabeth nodded slowly. "I think I understand it now," she said.

"And that's what I'm interested in doing with my art," Olivia concluded. "I'm only part of the way there, but I'm learning."

"I'm sure you are," Elizabeth said confidently.

For a few seconds, they sat in silence. Then Olivia shrugged and picked up her pencil again. "Better get back to work."

"Right."

Elizabeth was quickly engrossed in making notes for her weekly column, "Eyes and Ears." In theory it was a gossip column, but Elizabeth never used it to start or spread rumors. Of course, having the school's biggest gossipmonger for a twin sister meant that she *heard* all of the dirt. She just didn't print it.

"Hey, Liz," called a familiar voice from the doorway a while later. "Ready to go?"

Without turning around, Elizabeth raised her hand and nodded. Then she typed the last line for her column, pulled the paper out of the typewriter, and placed it on the desk.

"Hi, Jess," she said finally.

Jessica was strolling around the newspaper office, eyeing every reference book and pencil sharpener as though it were some strange, foreign object. She was still wearing the pink-and-white sweats she had worn to cheerleading practice. "Hi, Olivia," she said casually.

"Hi, Jessica." Olivia met Elizabeth's eyes briefly, grinned, and went back to her work.

"I'm all set," Elizabeth said, picking up her books. "Let's go. Bye, Liv. See you tomorrow."

Elizabeth followed her twin sister out of the office and they walked together down the deserted hallway. On the surface, they were as alike as two peas in a pod. Each girl had the same heart-shaped face, dimpled left cheek, and azure eyes, the same size-six figure and California tan.

But those who knew them well could tell who was who at a glance. Elizabeth's blond hair was usually pulled back so that it did not fall in her face while she was reading. Jessica wore her hair loose, allowing it to fly in the breeze while she played tennis or drove the red Fiat Spider convertible the twins shared. And while Elizabeth usually dressed in casual blouses and chinos, Jessica usually wore miniskirts, tank tops, and wild jewelry. Sharp observers could also notice that conscientious Elizabeth wore a wristwatch and Jessica did not. Jessica never cared what time it was. She operated on her *own* time.

But despite their differences, they were each other's best friend. Being twins meant they had a special bond and a special kind of understanding that no one or nothing could destroy.

"I *cannot* believe the way Olivia dresses," Jessica said as she pushed open the front door of Sweet Valley High and walked down the marble steps. "When is she going to get with it?"

Elizabeth laughed. "What are you talking about? I *like* the way Olivia dresses. She's unique."

"Come on, Liz." Jessica protested. "She dresses *weird*. I mean, half the time she looks like a hippie. Does she think we're still in the sixties or something?"

"No." Elizabeth opened the passenger door of the Fiat. "She has her own style, that's all. Maybe she doesn't want to look like everyone else. It's her way of expressing herself."

"That's my whole point," Jessica replied. "What she's expressing is, 'Look at me—I'm weird.' I mean, why would anyone deliberately not fit in? She looks like some kind of geek."

"Jessica!" Elizabeth said, exasperated. "Just drive. I don't want to talk about it anymore."

"That's because I'm right and you know it," Jessica said. She started the car and smiled angelically at Elizabeth.

Elizabeth sighed. Arguing with Jessica was pointless. She sneaked an affectionate look at Jessica and grinned. "You have the open-mindedness of a mule," she said.

"Thanks for the compliment, Liz," Jessica replied. "You always say the nicest things."

Elizabeth shrugged. "No problem."

"But listen," Jessica continued, completely unruffled. "Speaking of clothes—"

"I thought we weren't speaking of clothes anymore," Elizabeth broke in.

"*Speaking* of clothes," Jessica went on firmly, "I have this great idea."

Elizabeth frowned. "Uh-oh, I'm not sure the world is ready for another 'great idea' from Jessica Wakefield."

"This is an idea about how to make money for Christmas presents *and* get incredible discounts on clothes at the same time," Jessica went on, ignoring her sister.

"You sound like a bad television commercial," Elizabeth commented.

"Just listen to me for a second. I swear, this is a really great idea. We'll get temporary, part-time jobs at Simpson's department store! I saw

10

an ad in the paper that says they need extra help for the Christmas shopping rush."

Elizabeth was silent for a moment as she considered what her sister was proposing.

"Well?" Jessica demanded.

"I *could* use some extra money," Elizabeth began. "I need to buy a ton of presents."

"See? I knew you'd see it my way!" Jessica said. "Plus we'll get the store's employee discount."

Elizabeth laughed. "Knowing you, you'll probably spend every penny you earn before you even get your paycheck out of the store. Why don't you ask them to pay you in store credit? Then you won't even have to bother cashing a paycheck," she joked.

"That is an excellent idea!" Jessica cried.

Elizabeth rolled her eyes. "I was *kidding*, Jess."

"I told you this was a great idea," Jessica said cheerfully as she pulled the car into their driveway. "How can you stand having such a brilliant sister?"

"I like to think I get a little bit of reflected glory," Elizabeth said in her humblest voice.

Jessica giggled. "You do. So anyway, you'll find out all the details, see what we have to do to apply, and let me know, right? It's a sure thing!"

Elizabeth shook her head and opened the car

door. It was just like Jessica to leave all the "details" to her.

"Just you wait, Liz," Jessica said, linking her arm with Elizabeth's as they walked up to the house. "This is going to be the greatest job ever!"

Two

After finishing her work on *The Oracle*, Olivia took a bus to the end of her street and ran the rest of the way to her house. Her mother's car was in the driveway.

"Hi, Mom," she called as she opened the door. Olivia went into the kitchen, where her mother was unpacking groceries. "How was work today?"

"Busy," Mrs. Davidson said. "It seems as if people start their Christmas shopping earlier each year." Mrs. Davidson was the manager of the women's sportswear department at Simpson's.

Olivia took an apple out of a grocery bag. "I'm leaving for class early tonight," she said. "Can I take your car?"

"Sure, Liv. Just try not to get paint or charcoal on the upholstery, please," Mrs. Davidson asked with a smile.

Olivia gave her mother a kiss, grabbed the car keys, and went out to the garage. About a year earlier her parents had let her convert it to a studio. The familiar smells of oil paint, charcoal, and turpentine greeted her the moment she entered. To Olivia, the scents were as delicious as perfume. She picked up her portfolio and her box of equipment and hurried to the car.

When she arrived at the Forester Art School, Olivia parked the car and then headed to the school's gallery. The guard nodded hello to her as she stepped into the peaceful, spacious building.

"Where's the new display of student oil paintings?" she asked politely.

"Down the hall," the guard said, pointing to the left. "But it looks like a bunch of monkeys got into the paint, if you ask me," he added with a comical expression.

Olivia grinned and wandered down the hallway. Precise drawings from an architecture class lined both walls. They were skillfully done, but they did not really interest Olivia and she walked by with only a quick glance.

At the end of the corridor she stopped and looked ahead into a big room hung with abstract paintings. Some of the canvases were very large, and some were irregularly shaped. All were vibrant and glowing with color.

"Wow," she whispered appreciatively.

Olivia walked slowly into the room and critically examined each picture on the first wall. When she looked at one that did not immediately interest her, she tried to analyze just why it didn't. She knew that if the museum director had chosen it for this exhibition, it must be a good painting, at least in someone's opinion.

Olivia tried to determine if any of her recent paintings shared any of the qualities found in the ones in the gallery. Olivia *felt* as if she was doing good work, but she wasn't always confident. She often wondered if she was really doing something worthwhile or if she was just kidding herself and wasting time. The doubts were hard to ignore.

Olivia turned around to look at the pictures on the opposite wall and caught her breath.

"Oh," she gasped.

It was as if one of the paintings had called her by name. It was large and perfectly square, solid and self-assured. But the colors and lines splashed across the surface contradicted the painting's stability. They seemed to cry out for understanding and sympathy. Olivia was struck by the contrast, the tension of the work.

Olivia folded her arms and concentrated on

the painting. She was sure she would have recognized it as being exceptional even without having seen it hung in a gallery.

"So what do you think?" came a voice from behind her.

Olivia jumped in surprise and turned around. A young man from her painting class was standing beside her. His faded jeans and sweatshirt were smeared with paint, and he carried a beat-up portfolio and workbox.

"Sorry, I didn't mean to scare you," he said with a smile.

"That's all right." Olivia laughed. "I was completely spaced out."

The young man nodded his head toward the painting she had been admiring. "You like that one?" he asked.

"Yes, I really do," she said. "It seems so powerful to me. What do you think?"

"Well . . ." He propped his things against a bench and dug his hands into his pockets. "I think it works, but some of the colors look too clear to me, too definite. Maybe they should have been muddied up a little more. That might have given the work more of a feeling of uncertainty."

Olivia listened to the art student carefully. He seemed to know a lot about this painting. "Do you mean that if the painting wants to make a statement about uncertainty, it should more fully demonstrate that uncertainty in all of its elements?"

16

"Yes," he answered as he frowned intently at the picture.

"The problem might be with that yellow," Olivia suggested. "It's very sunny, very open."

"That's what I was thinking, too." Suddenly, he smiled. "Don't you sometimes feel that when you talk about a painting, it's as if you're talking a foreign language?"

"Maybe, but I like that," Olivia said. She looked at the painting again. "I want to know what this is called."

She stepped up to the little card posted on the wall beside the picture. "It's called 'Please #2,' " she read out loud. " 'By James Yates.' " Olivia turned around. "Is that you?" she asked hesitantly.

James nodded and smiled apologetically. "I didn't mean to be sneaky. I just wanted to get a totally honest opinion. People are usually so nervous about hurting your feelings that they don't tell you what they really think. Either that or they're brutally critical."

"Oh, I know," Olivia said, rolling her eyes. "The worst thing is when someone who doesn't really know what abstract painting is tries to give you an opinion on your work. You hear things like 'It sort of looks like a sunset.' "

"Oh, no!" James slapped his hand to his forehead. "Not a sunset!" They both laughed.

"So now that you know my name, how about telling me yours," James said, looking intently into Olivia's eyes.

"Uh, Olivia. Olivia Davidson," she said, feeling a little awkward all of a sudden. But that awkward feeling quickly faded as she and James continued their conversation. Olivia felt a warm glow of pleasure. Talking to someone who really understood what painting meant was wonderful. She was glad that she had responded so positively to James's painting. It made her feel that they had something in common.

"You didn't paint this in our class, did you?" she asked. "I'd feel like a jerk if I had never even noticed it while you were working on it."

He shook his head. "No, I did it at home. And besides, we're all concentrating on our own work in class. You shouldn't feel any pressure to notice anyone else's work while you're painting."

James sat on the bench and Olivia joined him. "Do you paint a lot at home?" Olivia asked him.

"That's all I do," James said, scratching at a splotch of dried green paint on the knee of his jeans. "I'm taking three classes here. See, I'm on a scholarship, so I'm spending as much time as I can painting now, while I'm getting some money." James laughed. "Still, sometimes I get the feeling I'll never have enough time to paint all the things I have inside my head."

Olivia nodded. She knew exactly what he meant. She had that feeling all the time.

"That one's good," James went on, pointing to a tall, narrow painting on another wall. "It shows a really strong movement of downward flow, but then those bright reds at the top pull you right back up again. It's full of activity."

Olivia studied the picture. It had not occurred to her to see it as a particularly active painting. But what James said made a lot of sense.

"You must spend a lot of time looking at pictures and thinking about pictures," she said.

James shrugged. "What else is there? I don't want to sound pompous or anything, but as far as I'm concerned, paintings are all that really matter."

"What about life?" Olivia asked lightly.

"Paintings *are* life," James answered seriously. "Everything else is unimportant—money, living in a fancy house, worrying about the little things."

"But don't you *have* to think about those things?" Olivia pressed. "You have to eat, don't you? And have a place to live."

"Sure. But those things just sort of get worked out somehow," James said with a shrug. "I believe that if I concentrate on my painting, everything else will fall into place."

Olivia groaned. "How can you be so confident?"

James shrugged. "I don't know. I guess I just believe in what I'm doing."

Olivia looked at James's paint-stained jeans

and faded sweatshirt. It was obvious he didn't care much about his clothes, anyway. And if he really had achieved the perspective he said he had, of not caring about anything except his art, she envied him. She could admire that, even though she was not at all sure she could ever reach that level herself.

Suddenly, Olivia's stomach growled loudly. She blushed and laughed sheepishly. "One of those little details—food—is really important to me right now," she said.

James grinned. "That's pretty bourgeois of you. You can't be a real artist and expect to eat, you know."

"Thanks a lot," Olivia teased as she stood up. "I'm not ready to be a starving artist yet, no matter what you say. I'm going to grab some dinner at the coffee shop. Do you want to come with me?"

"Sure." James stood up and patted his back pocket. He frowned. "Oh, wait. I must have left my wallet at home. Some other time, OK?"

Olivia smiled. "You really *don't* worry about the little things, do you? Come on," she said. "I'll split something with you."

"Well, thanks," he said. "But next time, I'll treat you."

Olivia picked up her portfolio. "Deal," she said. "Let's go; I'm starved!"

Olivia and James left the college gallery together and walked off campus to the coffee shop. On the way, Olivia asked James more questions about his ideas of painting. At one point he was so absorbed in their conversation that he stepped into a big puddle. Olivia opened her mouth to say something and then closed it when she realized he did not even notice that his sneakers were squelching noisily with each step. Finally, Olivia laughed.

"What?" he asked with a puzzled smile. "Did I say something funny?"

"No, I'm sorry." Olivia shook her head. "It's just that you're so into what you're saying and, well . . ." She looked down at his feet and grinned.

Slowly, James looked down, too. At last he realized his feet were soaking wet. He shook his foot and watched the drops fly off.

"I guess I got carried away," he said.

Olivia shook her head. "No, you were just really intense. I admire the fact that you have strong opinions and that you aren't afraid to come right out with them."

James looked at her quizzically. "Of course I have opinions. Don't you?"

Olivia shrugged uncomfortably. "I try to. I mean, sure, of course I have opinions, but I don't always feel comfortable expressing them. How do I know that my opinions are valid?"

"Opinions don't have to be 'valid.' Your beliefs belong to you. You can't be afraid," James said seriously. "You *have* to trust what you're doing. You have to believe in your own judgment."

Olivia frowned. "But—"

"Art isn't supposed to be easy, you know," James interrupted. "It *should* scare you. But you have to say, 'This is me, this is what I am.' And you have to make that decision yourself. You can't let someone else make it for you."

Olivia was listening to James so intently that she didn't notice that they had reached the coffee shop. They entered and joined the line at the cafeteria-style counter. Olivia sighed. Her mind was spinning.

"But then what's the point in going to art school?" she asked. "What are the professors there for? Why not just do your own work and ignore everyone?"

James put some napkins on a tray. "It's OK to *listen* to them. But you have to remember they aren't necessarily *right*."

"But they're professors," Olivia protested.

"So?" James shrugged. "We're *all* artists. What *you* have to say about my painting is as valid as what Mr. Cardozo has to say."

"Oh, I don't know." Olivia felt troubled and excited at the same time. Everything James said brought seventeen different responses to mind, but she couldn't seem to sort through them and find one that seemed really solid, one she really believed in.

Olivia frowned. "Just tell me, do you like tuna?"

"To paint?" James asked, sounding confused.

Olivia laughed. "No, to eat! For dinner."

"Oh." He nodded. "That's fine."

Olivia paid for their food and James carried the tray to a table. Olivia was no longer even sure she was hungry. She *was* sure that she wanted to keep talking to James, though.

"I guess the thing that worries me," she went on as she peeled the plastic wrap off their tuna sandwich, "is that you can think my response to your work is as valid as that of someone who has been painting and studying art for his whole life. I don't even know what *I'm* doing. How can I possibly know what anyone *else* is doing?"

James took his half of the sandwich and stared at it absently. "How can I think that your opinion matters as much as anyone else's? I just do." He took a huge, hungry bite.

"Then let me see more of your paintings," Olivia said, offering what she hoped would sound like a challenge. "And I'll try to think of something intelligent to say about them."

"Oh, no! Not intelligent!" James said through a mouthful of food. "Painting is not supposed to be an intellectual thing."

Olivia leaned forward. "But abstract expressionism started out as an intellectual movement, didn't it?"

"I don't totally agree with that," James replied.

"Then how do you explain a painting that is simply a field of white?" Olivia asked.

As she listened to James's response, Olivia found that one part of her mind was trying to comprehend all that James was saying, and searching for ways to express her own ideas. But another part of her mind remained detached from their conversation. That part was noticing how fascinating, unconventional, and attractive James was. It was admitting that she wanted them to have a lot in common. And it was hoping that they would be able to spend a lot more time together.

Olivia watched James closely as he talked and for a while she just let his voice wash over her. He represented so many things she wanted to be! Someday, she hoped, she would trust herself as much as he trusted himself.

Maybe, she thought, *if I hang around James, some of his confidence will rub off on me.*

Three

Olivia woke up the next day thinking about James, about how he could just be himself and not care what anybody else thought.

That was the attitude she wanted to have. *What difference does it make if people at school think I'm strange or unconventional?* she asked herself. *I'm going to continue to dress exactly as I want to, no matter how oddball someone might think it looks.*

"They can think whatever they want to," she said out loud, striding across her bedroom. "It doesn't matter to me."

Olivia looked at herself in the mirror. Her wild tangle of curly hair was like a cloud around her face. She pulled it up into a ponytail on the top of her head. Then she looked around for something to hold it in place.

On her desk was a stack of old 45-rpm records she had found in the attic. She leafed through them quickly.

Olivia smiled when she found "Ain't Nothing but a Hound Dog," by Elvis Presley. She twisted her ponytail into a rope and threaded it through the big hole in the record. When she let go, her hair fluffed out, holding the record in place. Who cared if it was a little bizarre to use a record as a ponytail holder? It was *her*.

From now on, Olivia decided, she was going to trust herself in her work, too. If she felt like painting a totally black canvas, that was what she would do. James had said that the important thing was for her not to let other people's opinions hold her back. Otherwise, she could become one hundred percent inhibited—frozen in place, afraid to move.

But she was not going to freeze. With a blissful sigh, Olivia spread her arms out and twirled in a circle. She was going to be free.

Still smiling, she finished dressing. The rest of her outfit consisted of a black leotard and leggings, a swirly pink-and-yellow chiffon skirt, and a blue checked vest. Stepping into a pair of black sandals, she smiled at her reflection.

"Perfect," she said.

She knew some of the girls at Sweet Valley High already thought she had a bizarre wardrobe. *But they haven't seen anything yet*, Olivia told herself gleefully. Starting today, it would look as if she had been holding back before. Starting today, she was going to follow her imagination down whatever path it led her.

Still smiling, she headed for the kitchen. "Morning," she said cheerfully to her parents.

"Good morning, sweetie," Mrs. Davidson said. But when she turned around, her smile froze in place. "What on earth?"

Olivia shook her head to make her hair bounce. "Like it?"

"Well . . ." Mrs. Davidson said. "I have to admit, I prefer your hair in a normal ponytail."

"Oh, Mom." Olivia sighed.

Olivia's father glanced at her over the top of his newspaper. "It certainly is *different*," he commented wryly.

"Should I stop by and visit you at the bank after school, Dad?" Olivia asked playfully.

Mr. Davidson, who was the manager of the Bank of California's Sweet Valley branch, pretended to be horrified at his daughter's suggestion. "Don't even *think* about it," he said. And then he grinned to assure Olivia that he was teasing. "Think of my reputation with the board."

"OK, you're off the hook this time," Olivia said as she took a seat at the breakfast table.

Olivia knew her father had been teasing. Still, she was pretty sure there was an element of truth in his remark. Both of her parents were pretty conservative. Mrs. Davidson was the type of woman who never left the house without first putting on lipstick. She always wore proper suits or dresses to work, and her hair was always carefully styled. Mr. Davidson wore a three-piece suit and a white shirt to work every day. His ties were as conservative as his suits, and his silk handkerchief was always perfectly placed in his breast pocket. Even his shoes were highly polished. Olivia sometimes thought there could not be a more conservative-looking couple in all of Sweet Valley.

But still, she was very grateful to her parents. In spite of how different Olivia was from them, the Davidsons encouraged her to do her own thing. They did not pretend to like everything she did or the way she dressed, and they were not shy about telling her so. But they had never tried to make her fit into their own mold. From the stories her friends told her, Olivia knew that a lot of parents were not so supportive. Olivia realized she was one of the lucky ones.

"Olivia," Mrs. Davidson began, "there's a sale on cotton blouses at Simpson's. Maybe you'd like—"

"No thanks, Mom," Olivia broke in. "You know I don't like anything in that store. Not even the socks."

"Not even the socks?" Mr. Davidson echoed.

Her mother winced. "But I thought—"

The telephone rang and Mrs. Davidson picked up the receiver with a slight frown still on her face. "Hello? . . . June! How are you?" Her expression instantly became brighter.

"I wonder what Aunt June is up to," Olivia said to her father as she poured herself a glass of orange juice.

She took a handful of cold cereal from a box on the table and munched on it dry as she listened to her mother's end of the conversation. Her mother's older sister, June, lived in Connecticut with her family. The Davidsons hardly ever saw them.

"Of course, we'd love to have you both," Mrs. Davidson was saying. "No, it's no trouble at all. I'm so glad Emily's thinking of schools out here."

Olivia pricked up her ears. Her cousin Emily had graduated from high school early, and was taking time off before college to get some work experience. From the sound of it, Aunt June and Emily were coming to visit so that Emily could check out some colleges in California.

"When are they coming?" Olivia asked, watching her mother eagerly.

Mrs. Davidson waved her hand at Olivia as a gesture to wait, and then nodded. "Wonderful, June. Then it's all settled. We'll see you soon. Bye-bye."

She hung up the phone and sat back down at the table. "Well. This is terrific," she said, picking up her coffee cup. "June and Emily are coming at the end of the week. Emily has interviews at several colleges up and down the coast, so they'll stay here and use Sweet Valley as a base."

"Great," Olivia said. "I can't wait to find out what Emily's like. I haven't seen her in ages."

"I'm sure she's a lot of fun," her mother said confidently as she reached out to pat down Olivia's hair. "Won't it be nice to have her for a visit?"

Olivia ducked her head away from her mother's neatening hand. "Sure. How long will she stay?"

"Until before Christmas," Mrs. Davidson answered. "June will stay for about a week to help Emily get oriented, and then she'll have to get back to work."

"That's great," Olivia repeated. "I can't wait to see Emily."

As she munched contentedly on another handful of dry cereal, the expression "looking at the world through rose-colored glasses" popped into her mind. It made her smile. But she really did feel that everything was rosy right now. The holidays were approaching, her cousin was coming for a long visit, and she had a new, fascinating friend in James.

Olivia whistled on her way out the door.

Jessica went to her usual table in the cafeteria at lunchtime. Her best friend, Lila Fowler, was already sitting there, sipping a diet soda and flipping idly through the pages of *Ingenue* magazine. She looked bored, as usual.

"Hi, Li," Jessica said, noticing the earrings her friend was wearing. "Are those new?"

Lila touched one of the gold hoops with the tip of one pink-polished fingernail. "These?" she drawled. "I've had them for ages. Since last week."

"Then you must be getting tired of them by now," Jessica said, teasing her friend.

Lila favored her with a long, languid glance. Lila was one of the richest girls in Sweet Valley. Not a week went by without her adding another designer piece to her phenomenal wardrobe. It was one of the things about Lila that Jessica admired.

It was also one of the things about Lila that drove Jessica crazy. It was impossible to keep up with Lila when it came to clothes and jewelry. Sometimes Jessica thought she should start playing the lottery. A big, multimillion-dollar payoff would finally put her in Lila's league—almost.

In the meantime, Jessica did what she could. And getting a job at Simpson's was a brilliant idea because it worked in two ways—it earned her money and it got her the store discount. Of course, Simpson's could not compare to the Beverly Hills boutiques where Lila often shopped. But at least it was some progress, Jessica assured herself.

"Do you want to go to the beach after school?" Lila asked, tossing her magazine onto the table.

"Can't," Jessica said as she bit into her sandwich. "I have a job interview."

"A *what*?" Lila gasped.

"You know, a job? As in working?" Jessica said patiently. "That's what those of us who didn't inherit a whole bankful of money actually *do*."

Lila shuddered. "Gross. So what company are you going to wreck this time?"

"Very funny." Jessica stuck her tongue out at Lila. She had worked part-time in the past. But just because she usually ended up bungling the job or hating it for some reason did not mean that she would make the same mistake again. Anyway, Jessica was sure that this time she had hit on the job that was just right for her.

"For your information, it just so happens that I have found the perfect career for me," Jessica said loftily. "I'm going into retail fashion."

Lila cocked one eyebrow. "Where?"

"Simpson's," Jessica said.

"Oh, *Simpson's*," Lila said with a patronizing smile. "It's such a *cute* department store."

Jessica narrowed her eyes. "Yes, I only work at *cute* stores," she said sarcastically.

"Oh, talk about cute," Lila said, suddenly leaning toward Jessica. "You will just *die* when

32

I tell you this. The owner? Mr. Simpson? He has the most dreamy, to-die-for son. His name is Robert."

Jessica felt a tingle of suspicion. "I never heard you mention him before. If he's so dreamy and to-die-for, how come you never went out with him?"

A pink blush stole across Lila's cheeks. "We just didn't hit it off, that's all."

"Oooh, what's this?" Jessica crowed. "Lila met a guy she couldn't get to fall at her feet?"

"Go ahead and laugh," Lila said haughtily. "I thought I was doing you a favor by telling you about him. But if you don't want to know . . ."

"Yes, I do," Jessica begged. "What's he like?"

Lila frowned. "Well, he's very corporate. He'll be going into the family business, of course."

"Uh-huh," Jessica said quickly. "But cut to the vital part. Does he have a girlfriend?"

"Not that I know of," Lila replied. "But I don't see him that often. I just run into him sometimes at the country club. He goes to a private school. He's a senior."

Jessica sat back in her chair and crossed her arms. Not only was working at Simpson's an excellent opportunity for getting new clothes, it could also be a fabulous opportunity for getting a new boyfriend. And a rich one at that. Jessica knew that Lila had high standards. If she said

Robert Simpson was a hunk, he was definitely a hunk.

"I think I'm going to like this job," Jessica murmured.

"You don't even *have* the job yet." Lila pointed out.

Jessica grinned. "Lila, give me some credit. I can *get* the job."

Lila laughed. "You're right. You can fool anybody."

Jessica was about to deliver a cutting reply when she caught sight of Olivia.

"Check this out," she whispered.

Lila followed Jessica's nod. The two of them watched Olivia walk over to stand on the lunch line. Jessica slowly shook her head.

"What is that *thing* in her hair?" Lila asked incredulously.

"Beats me." Jessica shrugged. "I think Olivia is going off the deep end. She thinks this is Greenwich Village or something."

Lila confidently smoothed down her designer skirt. "Well, all I can say is, if *you* ever dress like that, Jessica Wakefield, I will never speak to you again."

"You have nothing to worry about," Jessica said dryly.

Four

After school, Elizabeth pulled the car around to the front of the parking lot. She sat reading *The Grapes of Wrath* for English class while she waited patiently for her twin sister to appear. Job interview or no job interview, Jessica was always late.

"Liz, hurry up!" Jessica called out ten minutes later as she rushed down the steps toward the car.

Elizabeth rolled her eyes. "Sorry if I kept you waiting, Jess," she said.

"Let's just go. We're late!" Jessica jumped into the passenger seat. "This interview is so important. You have no idea."

"Sure I do," Elizabeth said. She grinned at

her sister and pulled out into the traffic. "I need this job, too, you know."

Jessica settled herself down and composed her face into an angelic smile. "But you don't know the most important part, Liz. Mr. Simpson—you know, the owner?"

"Yes," Elizabeth drawled. She had a pretty good idea what was coming. *There's a boy involved in this somewhere*, she thought.

"According to a very reliable source—" Jessica began.

"Lila," Elizabeth filled in, making the turn toward downtown Sweet Valley.

"Yes, Lila. She says Mr. Simpson has this very hot son who happens to be deeply involved in the family business." Jessica grinned. "Isn't that fantastic?"

"It's very nice for the Simpsons," Elizabeth teased. "I'm sure they're quite happy their son is interested in the family business. But what difference can it possibly make to you?"

"Ohhh! Sometimes you make me want to scream!" Jessica groaned.

"OK, OK," Elizabeth said. "So Mr. Simpson has this gorgeous son—"

"Gorgeous and very corporate, according to Lila," Jessica added.

"Whatever that means," Elizabeth continued. "So you're planning to make him fall head over heels in love with you and buy you everything in the store."

"Something like that," Jessica agreed.

"Good luck," Elizabeth said as she parked the car by the curb in front of Simpson's. "Here we are. And if you can get him to buy me a word processor, I'll be very grateful."

Together, Elizabeth and Jessica went into the department store and took the elevator to the top floor. When they stepped out, they were facing a large sign that said Store Personnel Only. A receptionist looked up from her computer.

"Hi, can I help you girls?" she asked politely.

"We have job interviews," Jessica answered, treating the receptionist to a dazzling smile. "I'm Jessica Wakefield, and this is my sister, Elizabeth."

Elizabeth was tempted to remind her sister that the receptionist was not the person who would be hiring them. *All that charm going to waste*, she thought.

"Fine," the receptionist said as she took two sheets of paper from a drawer. "If you girls will just fill out these questionnaires, I'll buzz the personnel office and let them know you're here."

Elizabeth took her form and walked over to an easy chair. She sat and began to fill out her name and address. Jessica sat on the edge of the next chair.

"Liz," Jessica whispered. "Try to look a little more aggressive."

"What should I do? Snarl? Or perhaps roar like a lion?" Elizabeth asked.

Jessica shushed her irritably and began to scrawl her name on her form. "Just let me do all the talking, OK? I really want us to get hired."

"Fine," Elizabeth said mildly.

"Elizabeth and Jessica Wakefield?" came a husky voice. A tall woman in a navy-blue suit had just entered the reception area. "Right this way, please."

Jessica popped up out of her chair and put her smile in place. Elizabeth followed her as the woman led them into an office marked Employee Relations.

"I'm Mrs. Endicott," the woman said as she seated herself at her desk. "Please sit down." She gestured toward two chairs in front of the desk, and Elizabeth and Jessica each took a seat.

"It's very nice to meet you, Mrs. Endicott," Jessica said perkily. "I want to start out by saying that Simpson's is my favorite department store. I've been coming here to shop for as long as I can remember."

Mrs. Endicott raised her eyebrows. "Well, isn't that nice. Now, you're both looking for part-time, temporary work, is that right?"

"Yes. Just during the holiday rush," Elizabeth explained.

"We *both* see this as an excellent opportunity

to start careers in retailing," Jessica gushed. "We may have to start out as temporary employees, but we hope that one day we'll work here full-time as sales associates."

"You certainly are go-getters, aren't you?" Mrs. Endicott commented.

"I like to think so," Jessica said brightly.

Elizabeth felt like sinking into the floor.

"I also want to say that I've heard such good things about how Simpson's treats its employees," Jessica hurried on. "I know the company has great corporate spirit, and I definitely want to be a part of that. And I don't think most people realize how vitally important the retail business is. I mean, Simpson's sells things people *need*. I think being part of that service would be really, really rewarding."

Elizabeth noticed that Mrs. Endicott seemed to be at a loss for words. *I guess Jessica's enthusiasm strikes her as a bit odd*, she thought.

"And do you feel that way as well?" she finally asked Elizabeth.

Elizabeth smiled sheepishly. "All *I* want to do right now is earn some extra money for Christmas presents," she admitted.

"Liz!" Jessica's smile was still in place, but her eyes looked very stormy.

Elizabeth returned her sister's bright but artificial smile. She knew she was spoiling Jessica's plan, but she really wanted to be honest with Mrs. Endicott.

"Elizabeth has as much team spirit as I do," Jessica insisted as she turned back to Mrs. Endicott. "She's just shy about showing it."

"Oh." Mrs. Endicott smiled faintly. "Well, has either of you had any work experience?"

"Yes," Elizabeth began, "at—"

"We've both held several different jobs," Jessica barged in. "We were candy stripers at the hospital, we've worked at our father's law office, and we worked as interns at the city newspaper."

Elizabeth resisted another smile. What would Mrs. Endicott think, she wondered, if she knew about Jessica's more disastrous job experiences?

"I'm very impressed," Mrs. Endicott said with a nod of her head. "I think we can find work for both of you right away."

"In which department?" Jessica asked brightly.

Mrs. Endicott consulted a computer printout that lay on her desk. "Well, we do need a lot of help in the stockroom of the children's department," she said. "Our inventory is coming in so quickly and everything needs to be checked and priced."

Jessica's face fell. "Oh, there's something else I wanted to mention. I thought that, well, because Liz and I are twins, you could use us in some high-visibility spot—you know, like at the perfume counter, or maybe in the scarves-

and-hat department, right by the front door. Don't you think people would be attracted by twins?"

"We'll see," Mrs. Endicott said with a faint smile. "Right now, though, we'll start you out in the stockroom and see how you do."

Jessica swallowed. "Gee, thanks. That sounds like a really great opportunity to learn the ropes."

"And we also need someone in gift-wrapping," Mrs. Endicott said. "How about it, Elizabeth?"

"Sure, I like wrapping presents," Elizabeth said.

Mrs. Endicott laughed. "Fine. You both start tomorrow, right after school. You can fill out the rest of your forms when you report for work. And welcome to Simpson's."

Elizabeth and Jessica stood up and shook hands with Mrs. Endicott. Then they left the personnel office and stood waiting for the elevator.

"Great," Jessica muttered, glancing furtively at the receptionist. "I get stuck in the babies' stockroom. Now how am I supposed to run into Robert Simpson?" She sighed dramatically and put her hand over her eyes.

"Maybe he'll be taking inventory, too," Elizabeth said. "You can always switch with me, you know."

"No way!" Jessica shook her head. "I've been in the wrapping department during the Christmas season. The people can be really vicious."

The elevator doors opened and they stepped inside. "You mean the gift wrappers?" Elizabeth asked, confused.

"No, silly. The *customers*." Jessica shuddered. "Have you *seen* the way they act? The stockroom sounds totally boring, but at least I'll be safe."

Elizabeth laughed. "I can handle the customers. Come on, let's stop in the sportswear department and see what we're going to buy with our first paychecks."

The elevator stopped on the menswear floor, and a young man in a suit stepped in. On his lapel was a tag that read Simpson's. He was a little older than the twins, and very good-looking. He stood facing the doors, with his back to the girls.

Elizabeth was startled when Jessica jabbed her with her elbow. She stifled a gasp and looked at her twin sister for an explanation.

Jessica widened her eyes and nodded toward the newcomer. "Robert," she mouthed silently. Her eyes sparkled with speculation.

Elizabeth looked doubtfully at her sister. *There is absolutely no reason for Jessica to believe that this guy is Robert Simpson*, she thought. *Unless hope counts as a legitimate reason*.

Jessica winked at Elizabeth. Then she took a

step closer to the young man. "Tommy? I *thought* that was you!"

The young man turned around in surprise. "Oh, sorry. My name is Max, not Tommy."

"Oops, I thought you were someone else," Jessica said with an apologetic smile. She stepped back next to Elizabeth and shrugged.

Elizabeth grinned. "Come on," she said as the elevator stopped on the sportswear floor. She had all she could do to keep from laughing. When they were finally out of earshot of the young man, she wrapped her arm around Jessica's shoulders and giggled. "You're too much," she said.

Jessica fluttered her eyelashes. "I know it."

"I'm going to look around," Elizabeth said. "Let's meet back here in fifteen minutes."

"Make it half an hour," Jessica replied.

Elizabeth wandered through the junior department and then into the sportswear department, mentally going over her Christmas list. She had a lot of presents to buy, and not just for her family. Her best friend, Enid Rollins, and her boyfriend, Todd Wilkins, were also priorities. She stopped and examined a stack of fluffy sweaters.

"Elizabeth?" a pleasant voice asked. "Or is it Jessica?"

Elizabeth turned around. "Oh, hi, Mrs. Davidson. It's Elizabeth. I'm starting my Christmas shopping."

"That's wonderful. I'm sure Olivia hasn't given it one thought yet. Sometimes I think that girl is living in her own dream world." The pride in Mrs. Davidson's voice softened the critical sound of her words.

"Olivia has much loftier things on her mind than shopping, that's all," Elizabeth replied. "She's thinking about Art with a capital *A*, and I'm thinking about whether I should get a blue or a pink headband for my sister. My concerns aren't exactly philosophical."

"There's nothing wrong with being considerate and thoughtful," Mrs. Davidson said firmly as she smoothed her already perfect hair with her hand. "Now, if you need any help, just let me know."

Elizabeth nodded. "Thanks—oh, and I'm going to be working here during the holiday rush," she added. "My sister and I just got temporary jobs."

Mrs. Davidson smiled. "Well, that's wonderful! I know you're going to love working at Simpson's."

"I'm sure we will," Elizabeth said politely. She waved and strolled away.

Talking to her friend's mother was always a little bit bewildering to Elizabeth. To Elizabeth's mind, there could not be a more totally opposite pair than Olivia and Mrs. Davidson.

And Mr. Davidson is as straight as they come, too, Elizabeth reflected. In a way, her parents' conservatism made Olivia's nonconformism stand-out even more. It was clear to all who knew her that Olivia was not just acting or pretending to be something she was not simply to rebel against her parents. As far as Elizabeth knew, Olivia loved her parents very much. She was just very, very different from them.

Olivia is an original, Elizabeth decided as she continued to wander among the display racks. She didn't let herself be pulled along by the crazy currents at Sweet Valley High. Maybe Jessica thought Olivia was from a different planet, but Elizabeth respected her for her honesty to herself.

But once in a while, when they were out with a bunch of other kids, Elizabeth caught a slightly troubled look in her friend's eyes. *It must be hard for her sometimes*, Elizabeth thought. *Olivia's probably very aware of how different she is, and that must make her feel uncertain at times*.

Elizabeth shrugged. It was just a suspicion she had. Maybe Olivia was totally contented and satisfied. Elizabeth glanced at her watch and headed back toward the junior department. She had just a few minutes left as a Simpson's customer. Starting the next day, she would be a Simpson's employee.

Five

Olivia walked into the grungy coffee shop and paused in the doorway. James had said he would meet her there at four o'clock. She let her eyes travel over the scuffed linoleum, the ripped vinyl in the booths, and the long, gray cafeteria-style counter with the solitary waitress wiping spots with a wet cloth. Olivia felt a rush of happiness. This was exactly the kind of place where artists hung out. It was authentically dismal and fascinating.

Then she almost laughed. She realized she had been looking at the room as though it were a movie set. But it was *real*. And she was part of it.

"Looking for me?" James asked, coming in behind her.

Olivia spun around. The moment she saw him, her heart soared. She was shocked at the intensity of the feeling.

Face it, she told herself. *You really like this guy.*

"Hi," she said casually. "Is this your home away from home?"

"Practically," James replied, ushering her to a booth. "The coffee is strong, the waitresses are crabby, and the toast is always burned. I love it."

Olivia grinned as she slid into the seat across from him. She noted that James's fingers were stained yellow. "What are you working on?" she asked, looking at his hands.

"A still life of bananas and daffodils on a sunny day," James said immediately.

Olivia widened her eyes. Then she burst out laughing. "Oh, sure."

"Actually," James went on, after they had ordered coffee and two slices of pie, "I was thinking of doing some oil sketches of the homeless guys who live in my neighborhood and calling the pictures 'Still Lives.' "

"Why?" Olivia rested her chin on her hands. "The men aren't still, are they? I mean, if they're homeless, they must wander around all the time."

James shook his head. "But don't you see? That's why they *are* still. It's like they've washed into an inlet somewhere, and they just float there, not really going anywhere."

"Would you paint them as figures?" Olivia asked.

"I'm not sure." James took a sip of his coffee and grimaced. "There's a kind of light that I always associate with homeless people, a sort of gray, winter-afternoon light. I'd try to capture that. And maybe the look of the street corners they call home."

Suddenly, Olivia felt a twinge of sadness. James's ideas sounded so good to her—so much better than most of the ideas she came up with.

"What's wrong?" James asked. "You have this strange look on your face."

Olivia blushed and stared down into her cup. "It's nothing. It's just that sometimes I think I'm really shallow. My ideas seem so stereotypical."

"Would you quit that?" James said seriously. "Stop cutting yourself down. I've seen what you're doing in class, and believe me, it's not shallow or stereotypical. And besides, you're still experimenting."

"Is it that obvious?" Olivia asked, curling her lip in self-mockery.

"I'm not even going to answer that," James replied.

"OK, I'll stop whining," Olivia said with a smile. "And I'll stop fishing for compliments. I know I'm young, I'm still in high school—"

"You're still in high school?" James interrupted.

"Yes." Olivia felt a flush of pleasure. "I thought you knew that."

"Then your work is even *more* remarkable," James said firmly. "All *I* have to think about is painting. You've still got stuff like trigonometry and American history nagging at you."

"Tell me about it!" Olivia smiled and suddenly found herself wondering what it would be like to kiss him. She blushed again and looked down at her untouched slice of pie.

Stop having such a one-track mind, she scolded herself. *Can't you just be friends with him because he's a talented painter? That's more important than romance.*

"Thanks," she mumbled, "for being so nice about my work."

"I'm not being nice," James said matter-of-factly. "I'm just telling the truth. I always tell the truth. Come on—if you've finished, let's take a walk."

Olivia nodded and gulped down the last of her coffee. As she put her cup down, her eyes rested on his paint-stained hands again.

"Seriously, though, what are you working on right now?" she asked. "Something for class?"

James put a few dollars down on the table for the check as he stood up. His eyes sparkled with enthusiasm. "Actually, it's something I'm working on for this new gallery. Do you want to see it? I live around the corner."

Olivia's heart leaped. "I'd love to," she said. "What new gallery?"

"A guy I know just opened it," James explained as they headed for the door. "He's putting on a show at Christmas, and if I can finish my painting by then, he'll put it in the show."

As they walked down the street together James told Olivia more about the gallery and its owner. And then he stopped in front of a television repair shop and gestured toward a door. "This is it."

"You live in a TV repair shop?" Olivia asked.

James laughed. "Upstairs. Come on." He pushed open a narrow door next to the shop and started up a steep flight of stairs. Olivia followed him.

At the top of the stairs, James fished in his pocket for a key. The door of his apartment was scratched and dirty, and a stale, oniony smell filled the hallway. Olivia was shocked at how dingy and depressing the building was. It was not the sort of place she had pictured James living in.

"Come on in," James said. He hit a light switch as he walked through the doorway.

James's apartment was one big room. The floor was bare. A rickety table stood with two mismatched chairs by it. Canvases were stacked against the walls, and an easel was set up by the window. Squashed tubes of paint lay on the window sill. One corner of the room was occupied by a small kitchenette. In the opposite corner sat an unmade bed. A lamp was placed on the floor next to it. Olivia realized with a pang that James was truly living on the edge. He had sacrificed the usual comforts of a nice home, for his work.

"This is it!" James said, striding toward the easel. "I just started today."

Olivia dug her hands in her jacket pocket and hugged her arms to her sides as she crossed the room. She hoped she would like the painting. She wanted to be able to say something positive, as though she had to justify the way he lived. She felt as though she had to say something that would assure James he had done the right thing in giving up so much.

Olivia stepped in front of the easel. The canvas was square, with irregular washes of yellows and gold slanted across it. Nothing at all came to her mind when she looked at it.

"It's, um . . ." she began.

"Don't." James shrugged. "It's nothing, so far. This is just the foundation. I can see the whole thing in my head. I know you'll like the finished painting."

Olivia looked at him and smiled. "It's a very nice foundation, though," she said lightly.

"Yeah, sure." James shrugged again. "Let me

show you some of my finished paintings." He walked over to the stack of canvases leaning against the wall and began to pull out several works.

Olivia watched him with a feeling of tenderness. James was not thinking about having a girl in his apartment. He was only thinking about his paintings. And his devotion touched her. Besides, she was strongly drawn to several of his paintings. They were bold and interesting, just like James. *Careful*, Olivia warned herself. *Remember, he's given no hint that he likes you as anything but a friend.*

"I think these are great," Olivia said honestly as she bent over to examine one of the paintings.

"Do you want something to drink?" James asked.

"Can you whip up a cappuccino?" Olivia quipped.

James made a wry face. "No, but I *can* make tea."

Olivia nodded and turned back to looking at the canvases while James put the kettle on. At one point, she glanced over her shoulder. James was just opening a cabinet, and she caught a glimpse of some cans of soup, a box of spaghetti, and a bottle of soy sauce. Other than that, the cupboard was empty.

"Here you go," James said a few minutes later. He held out a chipped mug to her.

"Thanks." Olivia sipped the weak tea slowly. She wondered briefly if she would be willing to live in the meager way James lived. She was not sure she would be.

"Let's go out on my deck," James said. He walked over to the window and opened it. Then he climbed over the paint tubes on the window sill and out onto the fire escape. He held his hand out to help her.

Olivia laughed as she stepped over the window sill to join him. "This is very elegant," she said. "And what a nice view of the back of that building."

They sat cross-legged, their cups of tea between them, and talked about their class. As each moment passed, Olivia felt more drawn to him. And she knew that if he appreciated honesty as much as he said he did, she could tell him that.

At last, Olivia finished her tea and took a deep breath. "James," she said, "I really like talking to you, you know that?"

"Me, too, Olivia," he replied. "You're very easy to talk to."

"Maybe . . ." Suddenly Olivia felt the way she did when she was about to jump into the cold waves at the beach. "I hope we can spend a lot of time together."

"Olivia," James said gravely as he set his mug down.

Olivia felt her heart sink. She had said too much, she realized. Her face got hot as he looked down through the bars of the fire escape.

"Listen, I like you a lot, Olivia," James continued. "But I have to tell you something right from the start. I can't get involved. I'm totally committed to my work, and that has to come before everything else."

Forcing herself to smile, Olivia looked at him and nodded. "I understand," she said. "But I *still* hope we can spend a lot of time together."

"So do I," he replied. "I want to be friends with you. That would mean a lot to me."

"Well, fine," Olivia answered brightly. She told herself that she was willing to accept his terms. She really *did* want to be friends with him. And if they were only friends, and nothing more, their relationship would still be a valuable one.

"Let's make a pact," James suggested. He reached in to the window sill and picked up one of the tubes of paint. He squeezed a dab of cobalt blue onto his finger, and then ran it lightly across her cheekbones.

"Hey!" Olivia laughed with surprise. The paint felt cool and sticky. Grinning, she picked up a tube of Naples yellow. "Where do you want it?"

He pointed to his nose. "Go ahead."

Olivia felt giddy with happiness. She reached out and smeared a streak of yellow paint down the bridge of his nose. "I think you should have some blue, too."

She put two blue dots on his chin, and James streaked yellow across her forehead. She felt that now they shared a secret sign. The paint on their faces was their badge of friendship.

"You should wear paint on your face all the time," James said. "It looks great on you."

Olivia could not stop smiling. *What difference does it make if James lives in a squalid, dingy apartment?* she asked herself. At the moment, it seemed like a castle with banners waving from every turret and trumpets blaring from the drawbridge.

"Here's to oil paint," Olivia said, raising her empty mug. "And I think I have to go now. It's getting late."

"Oh. Too bad." James ducked through the open window again and helped Olivia to follow him. "I'll see you in class the day after tomorrow, right?"

"Right." Olivia picked up her bag and walked to the door. She looked back for a moment. James's face was in shadow. "Bye."

Then she left and ran lightly down the stairs to the street. All of her senses felt alert as she walked down the sidewalk. She knew people were staring at the paint on her face, but she didn't care. She was alive and happy, and the paint was an important symbol of what she shared with James.

I'll never take it off, Olivia told herself.

Then she laughed. She knew she would take it off, but she also knew that, in a way, it would always be there. That knowledge kept her walking on air all the way home.

"Olivia? Is that you?" Mrs. Davidson called as Olivia walked in the front door.

"Hi, Mom!" Olivia went into the living room, where her mother was watching the evening news. She perched on the arm of Mrs. Davidson's chair.

"What on earth do you have all over your face?" Mrs. Davidson asked. "Is that oil paint? It must be very bad for your skin, Liv."

"Don't you like it?" Olivia grinned and touched the sticky paint with her finger. "I think it's pretty cool."

Mrs. Davidson sighed heavily. "If you say so, honey. Just do me a favor, OK? When Aunt June and Emily get here, try not to be quite so outlandish."

"Outlandish?" Olivia laughed. "That makes me sound like an extraterrestrial or something."

"You said it, not me," her mother teased. "Olivia, did you *really* walk around town like that?"

Olivia nodded. "I hate to have to inform you, Mrs. Davidson, but your daughter was seen in downtown Sweet Valley with oil paint on her face. Aren't you glad I didn't stop by the store to embarrass you?"

Mrs. Davidson got up and headed into the kitchen to start dinner. "Very. By the way, you'll never guess who was in the store today applying for temporary jobs."

Here it comes, Olivia told herself. *Mom's going to try to talk me into getting a part-time job at Simpson's again! She'll tell me it would be good experience.*

"Who?" Olivia asked.

"The Wakefield twins," Mrs. Davidson called back from the kitchen. "I think it's very enterprising of them."

Olivia restrained an exasperated sigh. "It sure is," she replied brightly.

Mrs. Davidson looked back through the door and smiled lovingly at Olivia. "Don't forget, Aunt June and Emily will be here tomorrow. So come home right after school."

"I will." Olivia felt a weight slowly settle on her shoulders. Sometimes her mother *did* make her feel closed in. But Olivia knew it was not deliberate. And she also knew that right now, at the most hectic time of the shopping year, her mother was under a lot of pressure at the store.

"I'll come home right after school," she promised again. "And I'll try to look like a normal person, I promise. Nothing *too* weird."

"Thank you, honey." Mrs. Davidson disappeared into the kitchen again.

Olivia shrugged. If her mother wanted her to look nice and respectable for their relatives, she would comply. Privately, however, she felt sure her cousin Emily would be the kind of girl who would *like* the oil paint symbols on Olivia's face. She had a strong feeling that she and Emily had a lot in common.

And she could not wait to see her.

Six

Olivia came straight home from school the next day. Her mother would be leaving Simpson's early to pick up Aunt June and Emily at the airport. There was still plenty of time for Olivia to get some work done in her studio before they arrived.

Olivia changed into her painting clothes—a black leotard and baggy drawstring pants—went into the garage, and began to prepare a fresh canvas. The cement floor felt cool and refreshing to her bare feet, and she hastily coiled up her springy hair and held it in place with a long paintbrush.

She could not wait to get to work. Spending time with James the day before had charged her imagination. She was bursting with ideas for new projects.

While she cleaned her palette with turpentine, Olivia let her mind drift back to the previous afternoon. Sitting on the fire escape, she and James had seen, through an open window, a woman cradling a baby in her arms. Olivia could still see them perfectly in her memory. At one point the infant had lifted up a tiny hand to touch his mother's mouth. Olivia's heart had soared.

The more she thought about the scene, the more convinced she had become that she could create a work based on the emotion of the mother and child. Her work would not be a figurative portrait, but an image of the love and tenderness. Olivia knew it would be an important painting for her to create.

Olivia slipped a tape of Mozart flute sonatas into her beat-up tape deck and began to block out the canvas in charcoal. Her arms felt loose and free, and the lines flowed into place as though they knew just where they were supposed to go. The painting would almost paint itself.

"Mother and child," she whispered to herself.

Before long, she was totally absorbed in her work. She used a wide, flat brush to lay on a ground of warm, glowing reds and pinks and peaches. Layer after layer built up on the canvas, the colors becoming more vibrant and resonant with each stroke of the brush. The colors almost seemed to pulsate, like the beat of a mother's heart.

A thick strand of hair fell down across Olivia's face, and she brushed it aside absently with the handle of her palette knife. She felt the coolness of a smear of paint across her cheek.

The picture was going to be good. She could feel it already. A powerful sense of serenity and pride washed over Olivia as she painted. Nothing else in her life but her painting had the ability to make her feel so good.

"Olivia?" Her mother's voice came faintly to her ears through the garage door.

Olivia came back down to earth with a jolt. The tape had stopped, and the wall clock told her an hour and a half had slipped away. Mrs. Davidson was back from the airport.

Olivia looked down at herself. She was a mess. But it was too late now to change. She quickly wiped her brush with a rag and ran into the house.

"Sorry, Mom. I was painting and I forgot to watch the time," she explained, hurrying into the living room.

"Olivia." Mrs. Davidson's voice held a note of disappointment.

Olivia smiled sheepishly, and looked eagerly at her cousin. Emily was wearing a khaki-colored suit and blue espadrilles. Her straight brown hair was held back by a plain blue headband. She held a briefcase in one hand.

"Hi," Olivia said uncertainly as she turned to smile at her Aunt June.

Her aunt and cousin looked at her with expressions of surprise. Olivia put one hand to her hair self-consciously, and the paintbrush that had held it in place suddenly fell out. Her tangled, paint-streaked hair cascaded around her shoulders.

"Hi, Olivia," Emily said as she put down her briefcase. "It's nice to see you again."

Olivia nodded. "It's been a long time," she managed to say.

"Nine years," Emily said in a way that made it clear to Olivia that she knew the time precisely.

Olivia rapidly searched her mind for something friendly and welcoming to say to her cousin. But she was too off-balance to think clearly. Emily wasn't anything like what she had expected. She looked like a junior executive.

"How was the trip?" Olivia asked finally. It wasn't what she had really wanted to say. It sounded so trite and conventional.

"It was fine," Aunt June said, retying her polka-dot silk bow tie. "Of course, we had called ahead to request the vegetarian meal, so that we would be served first. That's always the first thing on my checklist when I travel by plane."

Olivia laughed pleasantly. "Checklist! I'm lucky if I don't forget my wallet when I travel," she said. "Forget about making special arrangements." She smiled at Emily, but her cousin just looked confused.

There was an awkward silence. Olivia scratched her cheek nervously and found red paint on her fingers when she looked at her hand.

"Well," Mrs. Davidson said briskly. "Let's not just stand here. Why don't we all sit down?"

Olivia knew her clothes were too dirty for her to sit on the furniture, so she leaned against the doorframe. She felt incredibly clumsy and ill at ease, and that troubled her.

"So, Emily, do you have a plan of action for making your campus tours?" Mrs. Davidson asked.

"Sure." Emily opened her briefcase and took out an appointment book, several color-coded file folders, and a road map. "I have the whole thing worked out for the most efficient use of my time."

Olivia gulped. It looked as if her cousin had organized a state visit for a foreign dignitary! She couldn't get over how businesslike Emily seemed. She seemed even more conservative, by-the-book, and conventional than Olivia's parents were. At least they didn't use color-coded filing systems!

"I have one folder for each college," Emily

explained proudly. "In each one I've got their brochure, copies of my application essay, and a list of special questions I want to ask during my interview."

Olivia felt a flush steal across her cheeks. How could she ever be friends with someone like Emily? *She's exactly the opposite of me!* Olivia thought. She was not even sure she could have a *conversation* with Emily.

"That's very impressive, Emily," Mrs. Davidson said. Then she turned to Olivia. "Isn't that a terrific system?"

"It's great," Olivia said. Her voice sounded funny to her. She forced a smile to her lips and nodded. "Really great. Hey, why don't I get us some iced tea or something?"

Without waiting for an answer, Olivia hurried out of the room. When she reached the kitchen, she stopped for a moment to collect her thoughts. Everything was different now. The hopes and plans she had had for the holidays would have to be changed. Instead of going to parties with a fun-loving teenager, she would have to play hostess to a junior executive. Olivia knew that she was making a snap judgment of Emily, but she just could not help it.

She speculated for a moment on what snap judgment Emily was making about *her*. Olivia glanced down at herself: her baggy Indian-print pants tied at the ankles, her bare feet covered by spatters of paint, her hair a wild rat's nest. *I bet Emily thinks I look like an escaped lunatic,* she thought ruefully.

Olivia opened a cupboard and began taking out glasses. After arranging them on a tray, she poured out the iced tea and then backed up to the door to push it open. Olivia paused. She was not quite ready to go back out and face Emily and her briefcase and her file folders.

"I suppose you're smart to let her get all that out of her system," came Aunt June's voice.

Olivia's ears pricked up. Then Mrs. Davidson said something that she could not make out.

"But honestly," Aunt June went on. "Aren't you glad *you* put all of that foolishness behind you? Look at where you are now."

Olivia frowned. She had no idea what her aunt was talking about. What "foolishness"? But she guessed they had been talking about *her* before. The contrast between herself and Emily was probably just too strong for them to ignore.

A nagging thought scurried through Olivia's mind. *Was* she being too casual and frivolous about her life? She would never be as structured as Emily seemed to be. But perhaps it wouldn't hurt to start thinking about the future a little bit.

Then Olivia thought of her new painting, her glowing, radiant "Mother and Child." No, she was doing fine just the way she was, she decided firmly. Lifting her chin, she pushed open the kitchen door and went back to join her relatives.

Jessica reached down into the box and pulled out a bundle of pink crocheted baby sweaters. Gritting her teeth, she stacked them on a shelf and ticked off an entry on her clipboard.

"One dozen size newborn," she muttered to herself. It was her first afternoon on the job in the children's-department stockroom of Simpson's and already she hated it.

"Here's another delivery for you!" called out a cheerful voice. Tony, from the shipping department, trundled in a cart with three big boxes on it.

Jessica felt her shoulders sag. "Can't you take that stuff to housewares?" she begged. "I can't open any more cartons."

Tony shrugged apologetically. "Don't forget, it's the season to be jolly." He unloaded the hand truck and rolled it back out through the door.

"Ugggh," Jessica groaned. "If I find the guy who first said it's the season to be jolly, I'll deck him."

Her back was aching, her fingernails were dirty, and her feet hurt. So far, the exciting world of retail was anything *but* exciting. It was boring and backbreaking, and there wasn't anyone to talk to.

The door swung open again, and Tony came back through with another load.

"I'm not here!" Jessica said.

"Funny, you look like you're here." Tony laughed. "Hey, I was just talking to Robert Simpson. He asked who was working back here in the stockroom, so I told him it was a new kid."

Jessica stared at him. "You were just talking to Robert Simpson?"

"Yeah," Tony said. "He's a swell guy. Real friendly and polite to everyone. He's no snob."

Jessica tossed her clipboard aside, whizzed out the door, and ran full tilt into her supervisor, Mrs. Crawshaw.

"Sorry," Jessica gasped as she tried to see beyond Mrs. Crawshaw's ample shoulders.

"Are you going somewhere, Jessica?" Mrs. Crawshaw asked in a friendly voice.

"Excuse me, Mrs. Crawshaw," Jessica said as she tried desperately to squeeze between her boss and the cash register. The fact that Mrs. Crawshaw was standing as still as a statue was not helping to soothe Jessica's impatience. "I thought I saw a friend of mine."

"Oh, goodness, how foolish of me. You want to get by me, don't you?" Mrs. Crawshaw chuckled. "Sometimes I'm just as dumb as a post."

She moved her queenly bulk aside and Jessica sprang past her. She ran through the department, dodging displays of crib quilts and primary-color rattles, searching everywhere for her first glimpse of Robert Simpson.

But the only people she saw in the department were women, either holding little children by the hand or pushing strollers. Jessica skidded to a halt by a stack of fuzzy white teddy bears and blew her hair out of her eyes. Her quarry had made a clean getaway.

She was *never* going to meet Robert if she kept working back in that cave of a stockroom, Jessica realized grimly. And if her job was going to consist of nothing but opening boxes, counting baby sweaters, and making checkmarks on clipboards, she was going to require something more than just money in the way of compensation.

Meeting Robert Simpson was the one and only thing that would make the backbreaking boredom worthwhile.

Seven

Olivia and Emily cleared the dinner dishes, and as they did the washing up they carried on a stilted conversation about a movie they both had seen. Olivia knew she was not being very welcoming, and she felt bad about that, but she just did not feel that she and Emily had anything in common. For example, everything she had liked about the movie, Emily had not liked, and vice versa. Their tastes were at absolute opposite ends of the spectrum. It made talking to each other extremely difficult, even though Olivia could tell they were both trying hard to be friends.

"Why don't I help you unpack?" she asked as she wiped her hands on a dishtowel.

Emily had just finished separating the forks,

knives, and spoons into different compartments in the dishwasher. She smiled at Olivia. "Sure. Thanks."

"I tried to make enough room for you in my closet," Olivia said as they climbed the stairs. "I hope you don't think my room is too much of a wreck."

Olivia opened the door and stepped aside for her cousin. Emily carried her suitcase into the bedroom, and Olivia followed her in.

"It's, uh, it's nice," Emily observed after a moment of silence.

Olivia glanced around. Every wall of her bedroom was covered with sketches, photographs, posters, and clippings. Her desk was piled high with stacks of books, notebooks, drawing pads, clothes, and assorted junk. Her guitar was propped up on the desk chair. One string had snapped and was coiled around the neck like a broken spring.

"Here, let me move this," she said, squeezing by Emily and picking up the guitar. She shoved it in between a bookcase and her carton full of record albums. "So, welcome to my room."

Emily put her suitcase down on one of the twin beds. "Thanks. I'm glad you didn't go to a lot of trouble for me."

"No problem," Olivia said uncertainly. Obviously, Emily couldn't tell that Olivia had spent nearly an hour trying to bring order out of her usual chaos.

"You must spend a lot of time drawing and painting," Emily said, gesturing toward some of the works on the walls.

"*All* the time," Olivia agreed.

"Hey!" Emily said suddenly. "That's a really terrific picture!"

"Which one?" Olivia asked, pleased at Emily's reaction to her work.

Emily pointed to a pencil drawing of Mr. and Mrs. Davidson that Olivia had done in ninth grade. It was as meticulous and true to life as Olivia had known how to make it. It was the kind of drawing she rarely did anymore, and she only kept it because it was a portrait of her parents.

"I think that's the best of all of them," Emily said with an admiring smile.

Olivia returned the smile faintly. "Oh, thanks." She did not know what else to say. Emily's taste in art was as conservative as her taste in clothes. "Let me help you unpack, OK?"

"Sure." The clasps of Emily's suitcase sprang open with a snap, and Emily began to take out her neatly folded clothes.

"I emptied two drawers in my dresser for you," Olivia said. Suddenly, she imagined Emily's preppy blouses and polo shirts mixed in with her own tie-dyed tank tops and peasant skirts.

How would we tell whose were whose? Olivia asked herself with the beginnings of a wild laugh. She sat on the bed and told herself to be more patient. Just because Emily was not exactly like her didn't mean they could not still be friends. And it was petty and childish to make fun of her cousin simply because of her taste in clothes.

"So, where have you been working since you graduated from high school?" Olivia asked in a friendly voice.

"I've been doing temporary secretarial work," Emily explained. "I decided it was the best way for me to see firsthand a variety of different work environments and career options. Then I would have a better idea of what courses would be helpful to me in college."

"Oh," Olivia said. "That . . . makes a lot of sense." She picked up several of Emily's college folders and flipped one open. There was a list of pros and cons in Emily's neat, precise handwriting. It was cross-referenced with page numbers for the appropriate college catalog.

"This is really pretty amazing," she said, shaking her head. "Everything is so clear and in order."

Emily took a hanger out of the closet and shrugged. "That's just the way I am. I know sometimes it seems a little extreme, but it really makes things easier in the long run."

Olivia nodded and opened another folder. Her cousin was not just disciplined and organized, she was honest about it. Emily seemed to be really self-confident.

One entry on a list caught Olivia's attention. "Music? Are you interested in music?"

"The music industry," Emily corrected her. "It looks like an interesting field to go into if I decide to go to law school."

"Law school?" Olivia repeated. "How can you already know you might go to law school?"

Emily looked at her in surprise. "Well, don't you already have some idea of what you'll be doing after college?"

"I don't even have an idea about what I'll be doing after breakfast tomorrow," Olivia said. "So you have *everything* planned out?"

"Not everything." Emily sat down next to Olivia and picked up the stack of folders. She patted them into a neat pile as she spoke. "But I have a pretty good idea of what direction I'm headed in. I want a career that will allow me flexibility. If there are ups and downs in one part of the business world, I want to be able to switch to another. I'd like to get married at some point, too," she added shyly.

"To what kind of a guy?" Olivia asked.

Emily shrugged. "Oh, I don't know. But someone with real job security, someone I wouldn't have to worry about."

A picture of James and his shabby apartment popped into Olivia's mind. *Job security* was a term that just did not belong in his world. Olivia knew he was not interested in commitments, but, she wondered briefly, if she ever *did* have a long-term relationship with him, what kind of financial security *would* there be? The thought was a sobering one. She looked down at Emily's open briefcase again with a frown.

"Is this your high school transcript?" she asked, picking up a sheet of paper that seemed to be covered with A's and A+'s.

"Yes," Emily said. "I hope it's good enough to get me into the right schools."

"Good enough?" Olivia ran her finger down the list of extracurricular activities. "This looks like the combined efforts of three people, Emily. Hey," she added, "you worked on the school newspaper? So do I."

"Really? What do you do?" Emily asked.

Olivia crossed to her desk and picked up a pile of clippings and pages of frantic notes. "Arts editor," she said proudly. "These are some of my articles. I keep meaning to put them in a notebook, but I never get around to it."

She put the unruly pile in Emily's lap. Her cousin picked up a paper napkin covered with scribbles. "What's this?"

Olivia frowned at it. "Oh, notes from a school concert I attended. It was the only paper I had."

Emily nodded. "I was the copy editor for our

74

paper. You know, spelling, punctuation, fact-checking."

"Oh." Olivia felt her heart sink. No matter how hard she tried to be friends with Emily, they kept running up against a brick wall.

Olivia picked up Emily's transcript and looked through it again.

"This really is impressive," she said warmly. "I'm sure you won't have trouble getting into any college you want."

"I hope you're right." Emily smiled and went back to unpacking her suitcase.

As Olivia watched her cousin, she began to wonder again about her own lack of direction. Her high school transcript probably would not look very impressive. All it would show is that she had worked on the school newspaper and that she had taken a lot of extracurricular art classes.

Am I really aimless, just drifting through? she thought. Watching Emily place her carefully folded shirts in Olivia's dresser, Olivia felt a little bit sheepish. Maybe it *was* time to be a little less carefree and casual about everything.

"Hi, girls," Mrs. Davidson said from the doorway. "How's everything going?"

"Fine, Mom," Olivia said, still preoccupied with her thoughts.

"Olivia made plenty of room for me," Emily said as she hung up a gray suit.

"Oh, Emily, what an attractive suit!" Mrs. Davidson said. "I always hope Olivia will let me buy her a suit sometime, but she's very stubborn about it."

Normally, Olivia would have laughed off her mother's complaint as not really serious. But that night, she could not help but hear the underlying note of disappointment in her mother's voice. And she could not help but see what her mother saw—that in a lot of ways Emily was very impressive.

For one crazy moment, Olivia thought that maybe she *should* have a suit. It would certainly make her mother happy. And then just as suddenly she remembered who she was. She was Olivia Davidson, and Olivia Davidson did not wear suits. Even her considering wearing one was ridiculous. She shook her head and dragged her hand back through her wild, curly hair.

"Well, I'll leave you girls alone to talk," Mrs. Davidson said cheerfully. "Emily, let me know if you need anything."

"I will. Thanks." Emily closed her empty suitcase and slid it into the closet.

Olivia distractedly opened the folder on top of Emily's stack of files. She did not even see the colorful college brochure. Her mind was too far away.

"Do you know what colleges you might want to apply to?" Emily asked.

Olivia shook her head slowly. "No, I never really thought about it before." She realized how feeble that sounded. She really did wish she could be more focused about her own desires. "I think I'd like to go to art school, but sometimes I think I'd like to go to a regular college and take other kinds of courses, too."

"A liberal arts college," Emily supplied.

Olivia nodded. She had not even known the correct term for the kind of college she had in mind. "Right, liberal arts," she said quickly.

"Here in California, or somewhere else?" Emily asked politely.

"I don't know," she confessed, her shoulders sagging. "I guess I really do have to start thinking about it."

"Well, you probably should," Emily agreed. "It's never too early to start planning something as important as college. Going to the right college will make a difference to your whole life."

Emily's last words made Olivia feel worse than ever. She knew she was letting a harmless little conversation eat away at her self-esteem, but she just could not deny the truth of at least part of what Emily was saying.

"Listen," she said in an artificially bright voice as she stood up, "if you're all finished, why don't I show you my studio? That's where I spend all my time."

"OK, that sounds like fun," Emily said. "I've never been in a studio before."

"I'm taking a class at a local art college," she explained when they had reached the garage. "It's very exciting. All of the students are really into their work. I mean, it's not like a high school art class, where a lot of the kids are there just because they think art's an easy A." Olivia eagerly pulled some canvases away from the wall. "This is my favorite from last year," she told her cousin. "I think it's the best. I don't know how anyone else feels about it."

Emily walked over to Olivia, carefully avoiding the dirty, paint-covered easel and workbench. She looked at the painting with a frown of concentration on her face.

"What's it called?" she asked politely after several moments of silence.

"It's called 'Emily,' after Emily Dickinson," Olivia explained excitedly. "I read some of her poetry last year, and this painting expresses the way it made me feel. Do you like Emily Dickinson?"

"Well, her poetry doesn't rhyme very well, does it?" Emily pointed out. She bit her lip and looked again at the painting. "Is it, um, a portrait of her?"

Olivia looked down at her painting. There was no figure represented on the canvas. She had tried to capture the essence of Emily Dickinson, the lonely woman who had written such beautiful and strange poetry. As Olivia had worked, she had imagined standing at a window and looking out on a frightening and lonely world, just the way Emily Dickinson must have done all those years ago.

"Not really," she said slowly.

Emily blushed and shook her head. "Sorry. I don't know anything about art."

Olivia felt terribly embarrassed. She had babbled on and on about her work without even realizing that her words were going right by her cousin. She had not been able to communicate anything at all.

And her painting had not communicated anything to Emily, either. Olivia stood back and tried to see the picture through Emily's eyes. Did it look like a kid's finger painting or like aimless doodles on a telephone message pad? The painting said something to *her*, but maybe it was just meaningless gibberish to the rest of the world.

What am I doing with my life? Olivia asked herself, suddenly feeling empty inside.

Eight

Jessica picked up the little gun that inserted plastic price-tag holders into garments. Then she picked up another pair of booties and shot a tag into it.

"Take that," she grumbled.

She was so bored that she thought she would cry. And if she had to see another adorable romper or cuddly comforter, one more sweet-as-sugar sleep set or bouncy bath toy, she would scream. She had also vowed never to have children, or to be friends with anyone who had children. Although, at the rate she was going, she was never going to meet anyone new at all, with children or without. Working in the stockroom was the equivalent of being exiled to Siberia.

"That's it," she said, slapping down the price-tag gun. She *had* to get out of that back room. She strode purposefully to the stockroom door and pushed her way through it.

Out on the floor, throngs of people were pawing with grim determination through the merchandise. Mrs. Crawshaw was standing at the cash register, ringing up sales for a long line of impatient shoppers.

"Why don't I take over for you, Mrs. Crawshaw?" Jessica offered sweetly. "You look as if you could use a little break."

"Oh, Jessica, aren't you the nicest thing!" Mrs. Crawshaw gushed. "But you don't even know how to use the cash register yet, and besides, I couldn't put you through this kind of busy pace."

Jessica gritted her teeth. "I wouldn't mind at all."

"You're such a nice girl," Mrs. Crawshaw responded, punching numbers on the cash register so fast that to Jessica, her fingers were only a blur. "But I'm just fine. Oh, but would you be a dear and take these returns back to the stockroom for me?"

Jessica gave the long line of customers a sick smile, turned around, and trudged back to her own private torture chamber. No amount of money could make up for the agony of tearing open brown cardboard boxes and counting baby clothes all afternoon, every afternoon.

Now there was only one thing that was keeping Jessica from walking out on her new job: Robert Simpson.

Jessica had no doubt at all that once she met him, he would fall for her instantly. The problem was actually *meeting* Robert. Jessica sat down on a carton and propped her chin in her hands. *Maybe I was a fool to turn down the job at the gift-wrapping desk*, she thought. Because even if Robert Simpson never came by, there were bound to be *other* guys bringing their gifts to be wrapped. Jessica shook her head.

He'd better be worth it, Jessica thought grimly.

Elizabeth looked up as the next customer stepped forward. "Hi, Mrs. Brown," she said, recognizing an elderly neighbor. "How are you? I'm Elizabeth Wakefield."

"Elizabeth, what a surprise." Mrs. Brown put three boxed dollhouses on the counter. "These are for my granddaughters."

"Aren't they cute?" Elizabeth exclaimed. "I bet any little girl would love one of these. Which kind of paper would you like?"

Mrs. Brown looked at the huge rolls of colored wrapping paper hanging on the wall behind Elizabeth. "Let's see, how about the red paper with the jack-in-the-boxes and candy canes?"

"Excellent choice," Elizabeth said cheerfully. She ripped off a large piece for the first box and hummed along with the rendition of "Silver Bells" that was playing over the PA system.

"Those little girls are getting so grown-up," Mrs. Brown said. "It seems like only yesterday my own children were small."

Elizabeth smiled as she continued to wrap the dollhouses. No doubt about it, working in the gift-wrap department at Christmastime was hectic. But it was fun, too. People were so happy when they had found the perfect present for someone they loved. And she had had the opportunity to see a lot of friends and neighbors, too. Elizabeth tied special bows for the three packages and smiled warmly at Mrs. Brown.

"Merry Christmas," she said.

A young woman stepped up to the counter next and presented a pair of high-tech ski goggles. "Can I have that really cool iridescent paper, please?" the customer asked.

"Sure." Elizabeth examined the goggles quickly. They would be the perfect gift for Todd.

Working in the wrapping department meant that, in a way, the store came to her. Already she knew just what she would get for her parents, her brother Steven, and her grandparents. And she hadn't even had to go looking!

Elizabeth placed a silver Simpson's sticker on the package. Then she looked at her watch. Her shift was almost over.

"Thank you for shopping at Simpson's. Have a nice holiday," she said to the customer.

"Hi, Elizabeth," said Janet, the woman whose shift was about to start, as she came through the gate in the gift-wrap desk. "Busy today?"

"Very." Elizabeth took a deep breath. Her shoulders were tense. "I'll see you tomorrow. Bye!"

Gratefully, Elizabeth escaped from behind the desk and headed for the escalators. She was supposed to meet up with Jessica so they could drive home together.

Several steps above her on the escalator was a familiar figure. Elizabeth knew she would have recognized that mop of curly hair anywhere, even without the batik jumper and black T-shirt as confirmation. She climbed ahead a few steps and tapped Olivia on the shoulder.

"Howdy," she said.

Olivia turned around with a start. "Oh, Liz. Hi."

"Doing your Christmas shopping?" Elizabeth asked her friend. They reached the next floor and stepped off the escalator.

Olivia gave her a mock horrified look. "Me? Shop at Simpson's?"

"Oh, right." Elizabeth laughed. "How could I even suggest such a crazy thing?"

"I'm just picking up my mother," Olivia explained. Suddenly, her smile faded into a slightly thoughtful expression.

"Are you OK?" Elizabeth asked quietly.

"Sure, I'm fine." Olivia tried to look cheerful as they walked past a Christmas display. "It's just that . . ."

Elizabeth swung her friend's arm back and forth. "Come on," she coaxed. "Tell me what's wrong."

"Well, it's sort of silly, actually. See, my cousin is staying with us while she goes on her college interviews," Olivia explained. "And it seems as if she's got everything—her whole life—so thoroughly planned out. It's been making me wonder if I'm just goofing off."

"Goofing off?" Elizabeth repeated. "Come on, how can you say something like that? You're busy all the time, painting, writing, pursuing your interests."

"Yeah, but maybe my interests aren't very practical," Olivia countered.

"Well, who ever said art was supposed to be *practical*?" Elizabeth asked. "It's supposed to feed the spirit, not the hungry."

Olivia stopped in front of a trio of mannequins dressed for a New Year's Eve party. "I guess it depends on who it is that's hungry," she said softly.

"What?" Elizabeth looked at her friend quizzically. "Olivia, come on. We're only juniors in high school. We have a lot of time before we need to start thinking about being really practical."

Olivia shrugged and smiled. "You're right, I guess. Look, I have to go. I'll see you in school, OK?"

"Sure. Bye." Elizabeth watched Olivia head solemnly for the sportswear department, and hoped that whatever it was that was really bothering Olivia would not ruin her Christmas.

Olivia walked slowly through the sportswear department. She glanced at the displays of brightly colored polo shirts, warm-up suits with brand names splashed across them, and pretty cotton sweaters. Every Christmas Mrs. Davidson optimistically picked out at least one outfit from this department for Olivia. The fact that Olivia never wore the clothes never deterred Mrs. Davidson from trying again the following year. Olivia stopped by a rack of denim skirts and slowly shook her head.

"Sorry, Mom," she whispered. "This is just not me."

Olivia wove her way through the racks and shelves to a door marked Staff Only. She knocked, then pushed it open and went in.

"Olivia," Mrs. Davidson said, looking up from her desk in surprise. "Is it time to go?"

"Time to go, Mom," Olivia said, taking a seat across from her mother.

"Well, I'm almost ready. I just have to check this list once more." Mrs. Davidson returned her attention to the papers on her desk.

The desk was always neat, in spite of Mrs. Davidson's heavy workload. In a pretty silver frame was a photograph of Olivia wearing an off-the-shoulder Mexican blouse, dangling silver earrings, and a blue-and-black striped shawl. Olivia was touched that her mother would pick out that particular photo to have on her desk.

Olivia looked around her mother's office. On the walls were framed commendations, an employee-of-the-year certificate, and pictures of her mother with Mr. Simpson. Olivia knew her mother was proud of her job.

And Olivia was proud of her mother. It was just that her mother's choice of career seemed so alien to her. She simply couldn't imagine dressing up every morning, reporting to the same office at nine o'clock, performing basically the same routine day in and day out, year in and year out. The thought of it made Olivia shudder.

"Emily's sweet, isn't she?" Mrs. Davidson said suddenly, breaking into Olivia's thoughts.

"Oh, sure." Olivia nodded.

"She's very nice, and so organized," Mrs. Davidson went on. "You don't see a lot of girls her age who are so clear about their plans."

Olivia felt her shoulders tightening. She knew what this was leading up to. "No, it's pretty unusual, Mom," she answered.

"Did she tell you some of the companies she's worked for?" her mother continued. "Some very impressive places, branch offices of big corporations."

"Yeah, really great," Olivia answered tightly.

Mrs. Davidson took her glasses off and folded them up. "You know, Olivia, it wouldn't hurt *you* to get some practical work experience. It would give you a chance to see what kind of career you might want."

"Mom, I want to be a painter," Olivia said.

"Oh, I know that, honey," Mrs. Davidson said warmly. "But what about a *job*?"

Olivia looked down at her lap. Her heart was pounding. Her mother's words bothered her more than she had thought they ever could.

"I was thinking," her mother went on, "that you could get a part-time job here. I know I could arrange it for you with Mrs. Endicott in personnel."

Olivia looked up in astonishment. "Me? Work *here*?" Immediately, she regretted her words. Mrs. Davidson looked hurt. Olivia gulped hard.

"It's good enough for me," Mrs. Davidson said lightly.

"I know. That's not what I meant, Mom," Olivia said. "I didn't mean to insult you."

Her mother nodded tiredly. "I know you think that what I do here is hopelessly boring and middle-class. But I enjoy working here and I think you might, too, if you'd only try it."

"Mom, I just don't—" Olivia stopped herself and took a deep breath. She felt very depressed. "Can we talk about this some other time? It's getting late."

"Of course." Mrs. Davidson packed her briefcase and then put on her coat. "Let's go home. Emily had her interview at UCLA today, and I'm looking forward to hearing about it. Aren't you?"

Olivia felt a sinking sensation in her stomach. "The interview probably went *perfectly*. I bet they loved her and can't wait to accept her."

"What does that mean?" her mother asked.

"What? It means what I said."

Mrs. Davidson shook her head. "Your tone of voice certainly wasn't very nice."

"I didn't—" Olivia closed her eyes for a moment. She felt stifled by her mother again. She hated to feel this way, because she loved her mother. "If I used a funny tone of voice, I'm sorry. I really think Emily is a great candidate for any school. And I really wish her good luck."

"You should tell her that," her mother said. "Listen, I have an idea. Why don't you take Emily somewhere after dinner, to one of those places you and your friends like to go?"

"But I'm meeting James Yates later on, that guy from my painting class," Olivia said quickly.

"Is it a date?" Mrs. Davidson asked.

Olivia felt her cheeks grow warm. She knew all too well that it wasn't a date. James had made his feelings quite clear on that score.

"No," she answered. "We're just having coffee."

"Then you *could* take Emily with you, Olivia," her mother said. "It would be the friendly thing to do."

Olivia gave up. She knew she had hurt her mother's feelings this afternoon. She knew she was a disappointment in a lot of ways.

"OK," she said, even though she knew instinctively that Emily and James would not be a good combination. "I'll ask her if she wants to go."

Nine

Olivia got into the car after dinner and unlocked the passenger door so Emily could scoot in. She smiled hesitantly at her cousin.

"It's just a grungy old coffee shop," she said, hoping Emily would back out. "It's nothing special."

"That's OK," Emily said cheerfully. "Besides, I'd like to meet your friend."

"Sure. I should warn you, though: James has a one-track mind."

Emily buckled her seat belt and smoothed down her khaki pants. "Which track?" she asked with a smile.

"All he talks about is art," Olivia said, still hoping to discourage her cousin from joining them. "He never even *thinks* about anything else."

"Don't worry," Emily said. "I'm sure I'll like him."

Olivia shrugged and started the car. She *was* worried. She was worried that James wouldn't like Emily, and that Emily wouldn't like James. Why *would* they like each other? she asked herself. They had absolutely nothing in common.

"OK, but don't say I didn't warn you," Olivia said as they drove down the street. "The coffee shop isn't fancy or anything. I mean, sometimes the silverware is clean and sometimes it isn't."

"Are you *serious*?"

Olivia smiled. "Well, not really. But you get the picture."

For the rest of the ride, Emily told Olivia about her interview at UCLA. Olivia only half listened. Her mind was on James. In spite of what he had said about commitments, she knew she was practically in love with him. And she couldn't wait to see him.

"This is it," she said a little while later, pulling up to the curb.

Emily looked doubtfully through the car window. "This is it, huh? Well, OK. It'll probably turn out to have the best coffee in California or something like that."

Olivia led the way inside and quickly glanced around the restaurant. The booths were filled with people huddled over cups of coffee or plates of hamburgers and greasy fries. Cigarette smoke coiled through the air, and the cook was fiddling with the vertical hold on the TV above the counter. Someone let out a loud guffaw and then started coughing.

"Is he here?" Emily asked.

Olivia spotted James in a booth in the corner. "He's over there," she answered, and started to walk toward him.

"Hi, James," she said as she slid into the seat.

James looked up at her, his eyes bright and welcoming. Then he looked surprised as Emily sat down, too.

"James, this is my cousin Emily," Olivia said. "She's staying with us while she goes on her college interviews."

"How do you do?" Emily asked, holding out her hand.

James looked at her hand and then shook it slowly. "How do I *do*?" he repeated in a surprised voice.

"He do fine," Olivia teased.

"I hear you're really into art," Emily said in a perky voice when she and Olivia had ordered coffee and donuts. James ordered only coffee.

"Into art?" James said.

"You're beginning to sound like an echo," Olivia told him with an uncomfortable laugh.

"Sorry," James said. "Yeah, I'm very involved in my work."

Emily nodded. "Oh, you work, too? Olivia

said you were a painter. She didn't say you also had a job."

"Painting is my work," James explained.

"Oh, I'm sorry, I thought—" Emily blushed. "Now I really feel dumb."

Olivia gave her cousin a weak smile. "No, don't. A lot of people don't think of painting as work."

"Well, I don't really know anything about art," Emily admitted. "I have been to the Metropolitan Museum of Art in New York City, though. I really like Manet. He did those pretty gardens and cathedrals and water lilies, right?"

Olivia felt a sting of embarrassment. "That's Monet," she corrected. Just then the waitress brought their coffee and donuts. She plunked everything down so hard that the donuts almost bounced off the plates. When the waitress had gone, Emily wiped a spot of dried egg yolk off her spoon.

"Monet was nearly blind," James said abruptly. "That's why he painted the way he did. I can't particularly admire him for the way he painted, because it wasn't a conscious choice. It was just the way he saw."

"But isn't his vision just as valid as yours?" Olivia argued. "I mean, the artist's vision is the artist's vision. What difference does it make if he needed glasses? He painted what he saw and you paint what you see."

"I still think he's given too much credit for

starting a movement when he had no intention of starting one. It was almost an accident, really."

"A lucky accident," Olivia insisted. "Some of his last paintings were actually examples of abstract expressionism. Because he could hardly see anything, he was painting what was in his head."

Emily cleared her throat. Olivia and James turned toward her and Olivia realized with a guilty pang that she had forgotten all about her cousin.

"Oh, sorry," Olivia said.

"That's OK," Emily said. "It was really interesting."

An awkward silence descended on the table. Olivia fiddled with the salt shaker.

"So—" she began.

"I heard this—" James said at the same time.

Olivia nodded. "Go ahead."

"No, it was nothing," he said, shaking his head and picking up his coffee cup.

Emily looked around the coffee shop. "Do you come here a lot?" she asked.

"I live around the corner," James explained. "And besides, it has the cheapest food around."

Laughing, Emily said, "Sometimes it's worth spending a little money, though, isn't it?"

"Not if you don't have any," he replied simply. "I paid my rent today, so now I'm broke. I can't even buy a new tube of white paint until

I get my stipend check from the college next week."

Olivia felt her heart plunge. She looked at the coffee in front of him and knew why he hadn't ordered anything to eat. He couldn't afford to.

Suddenly she was overcome with feelings of tenderness and protectiveness. She wanted to put her arms around James. It wasn't fair that he should have to suffer so much to follow his dreams. More than ever, she wished Emily weren't sitting at the table with them. It was impossible for her to speak openly to James about what she was feeling.

"Listen, I didn't mean to sound so depressing," James said quickly. He smiled and shrugged. "It's the price you pay, you know? I don't mind."

"I guess I'm lucky I'm interested in business instead of art or music or something like that," Emily said.

"Well, somebody has to get rich and spend their money on artists," Olivia pointed out, half-jokingly. It was true. Someone like Emily might be in a position to buy a painting someday. But would she buy a *painting*, or would she rather spend her money on fur coats or sports cars?

"Maybe I could see some of your paintings sometime," Emily said to James. "I might like them."

"They're much better than mine," Olivia said. "His work is terrific."

James looked pleased. "The new picture is really getting somewhere," he told Olivia. "I'm using a foam brush."

"Why?" Olivia asked. "No brush marks?"

"Right," he said, hunching over his coffee. "Part of the canvas is going to be as clean as possible. But there will be parts where the paint is heavy, and the brush marks are right there."

"Have you ever seen Drokowski's work?" Olivia asked eagerly. "She had some pictures at the museum in L.A. last spring and she—"

Emily's puzzled expression pulled Olivia up short. She gave her cousin a rueful look. "Sorry. This must be really boring for you."

"No, it's fine," Emily protested.

James stood up. "Listen, I have to go, anyway. I have to get some work done tonight."

Olivia knew that James would have stayed longer if they had been alone. But there was no use in wishing for something that could not be. She nodded.

"It was really nice meeting you," Emily said, giving James a friendly smile.

"Same here," he replied. He looked at Olivia again. "I'll see you in class."

"Bye," Olivia answered softly.

The two girls sat in silence until James had gone. Emily dunked her donut carefully in her coffee and let the excess drip off in her cup before taking a bite. Olivia toyed with her cup.

"He's very interesting," Emily said suddenly.

"I know," Olivia agreed.

"But," Emily said, shaking her head, "what a way to live. Do you think he really meant it when he said he had no money at all?"

Olivia nodded. "He meant it. He never hides anything or tries to make excuses for what he does."

"That's good, I guess," Emily said doubtfully. "What is he going to do after art school?"

"I don't know," Olivia admitted. "He probably just plans to paint."

"But his stipend from the college will end," Emily pointed out. "He'll have to make a living somehow. He doesn't have a job that makes him money, right?"

Olivia nodded. In her mind's eye she saw James's bleak apartment: the empty cupboards, the ugly, clumsy furniture. There was nothing beautiful or artistic in that apartment. It was no way to live. "I guess he'll find a way to get by," she said, though not at all convinced by her words.

"Well, it's just not very practical," Emily said. "I mean, I know art is important, but so is eating, so is having a place to live, so is being able to afford medical insurance. You can't just ignore those things."

"I know," Olivia said feebly. Her face felt flushed. "I know," she repeated in a whisper.

Everything Emily said made perfect sense. Still, Olivia had a feeling that she had to defend James. And she did not quite know why. Maybe James *was* being too idealistic. Maybe he assumed someone would come to his rescue because he deserved it as an artist.

But nobody *was* coming to his rescue. *He really should be trying to fend for himself,* Olivia thought. *For his own good,* she added quickly, to quell some of the disloyalty she suddenly felt. *How can he be so short of money that he can't even afford paint and still not try to find a way out?* Emily was right. He was impractical, and probably pretty stubborn, too.

"He should at least learn a trade, like plumbing or electrical wiring," Emily went on. "Those jobs pay really well and he could take jobs only when he needed the money."

Olivia twitched her shoulders uncomfortably. The conversation was getting too depressing because it kept bringing her back to the question that had been nagging her since Emily's arrival: What was *she* going to do with her life in the future? She, too, was nearly broke right now, and didn't know how she would be able to buy the new set of brushes she had her eye on. She knew she could not keep asking her parents for money. It wasn't fair, and it wasn't responsible. *Maybe it's time I started facing reality, too,* Olivia thought.

"Are you finished?" Olivia asked, standing up abruptly. "Let's go."

By the time they got home, Olivia was feeling gloomy. She knew it was foolish to romanticize the life of an artist. She had seen the way James lived, and it wasn't very romantic at all. Going hungry and worrying about money all the time was *not* the way Olivia wanted to spend her life.

Olivia stopped by her parents' bedroom on the way to her own. Mrs. Davidson was hanging up some clothes.

"Hi, Olivia," she said. "Did you girls have a good time?"

Olivia sat on the edge of the bed and bit her lip nervously. "Yeah, it was fine. Mom, I was wondering. Do you think I could still get a job at Simpson's?"

"Do you mean it?" Mrs. Davidson asked with a beaming smile. "You're really interested?"

"I need the money," Olivia said morosely.

"I'm so glad you're finally taking an interest in working. I'll tell you what I'll do." She sat down next to Olivia and took her hand. "I'll talk to Mrs. Endicott first thing in the morning. If she has a place for you, I'll leave a message at school and you can start work tomorrow afternoon."

"Great," Olivia said, trying to put some enthusiasm into her voice.

Mrs. Davidson smiled lovingly at Olivia. "You should wear something nice to school tomorrow. Something plain and simple, OK?"

Olivia nodded. She desperately wanted to believe she was doing the right thing.

"That'll be great," she said again as she gave her mother a hug. "Thanks a lot, Mom."

"You'll see, sweetheart," Mrs. Davidson said. "This is going to work out just fine. You'll see."

Ten

Olivia went to the administration office at lunchtime the next day.

Please don't let it work out, she prayed silently. *Please don't let there be any openings at Simpson's!*

Then she remembered the squalid, hand-to-mouth way James was living, and she told her doubts to shut up.

"Hi, I'm Olivia Davidson," she said to one of the secretaries. "Is there a message for me?"

"Davidson . . ." The woman leafed through a stack of pink slips. "Yes, here it is."

Olivia glanced down at the message. It read, *All set. You can start right after school. Report to Mr. Jenner in menswear. Mom.* She crumpled the note and stuffed it in her backpack. Starting that afternoon, she was going to be practical.

It's the right thing to do. It is, she told herself sternly. *It's time to face facts and start thinking about my future.*

Olivia took the bus downtown after school, and got out a block away from the department store. As she strode quickly toward the main entrance, she sneaked a few quick glances at her reflection in the plate-glass windows.

She decided she looked pretty conservative, relatively speaking. Following her mother's advice, she had picked her outfit with Simpson's in mind. She wore a pleated, multicolored chiffon skirt and a white blouse with long, billowing sleeves and a large collar. She had pulled her fluffy hair away from her face with a twisted green scarf.

"This is as straight as it gets," she muttered. Then she squared her shoulders and walked into the store.

At once, the familiar sensation descended on her. Simpson's was a shrine to consumerism, with enough goods for sale to dazzle even the most blasé shopper. Olivia frowned and tried to put thoughts like that behind her. Simpson's was now her employer, her passport to the brushes, paints, and canvases she needed to pursue her real passion.

"Hi, I'm looking for Mr. Jenner," Olivia said

to the first sales assistant she saw in the menswear department.

The assistant was a young man in an impeccable gray suit. He gave her a friendly smile that extended to the expression in his brown eyes.

"He's in his office," the young man said. "Take a left at silk ties, straight past wallets, and you'll see the door."

Olivia smiled. "Thanks. I'm starting work here," she told him in a stage whisper. "I'm Olivia."

"My name is Robert," he replied. "Jenner's tough, but he won't bite."

"Thanks for the tip," Olivia said. "I'll see you later."

Taking a deep breath, Olivia headed for the tie counter and took a left. Straight ahead was a door marked Staff Only.

"Come in," a gruff voice said in answer to her knock.

Olivia opened the door. "Mr. Jenner? I'm Olivia Davidson. I think—"

"Yes, yes," Mr. Jenner said brusquely. He was a thin, balding man with a pinched expression. "Another case of pulling strings. Some people get jobs handed to them, not like others who have to *work* for what they get."

Olivia gulped. "I'm not trying to take advantage of my mother's position, Mr. Jenner."

"Hmm." Mr. Jenner tightened the knot of his

blue-and-red striped tie. "I don't know why they send them all to me," he muttered.

Olivia was at a loss for words. She didn't know why her supervisor was so bitter, and she wasn't sure she wanted to know. But she *did* know that she already had a black mark against her. She would have to make a real effort to prove to him that he was wrong about her.

The silence became embarrassing. Olivia gestured toward the door. "Should I ask Robert to show me what to do?" she asked nervously.

"Robert? Hmph! I figured you would know him," Mr. Jenner said. "Robert Simpson, the company prince. Thinks he's already the boss."

Warning bells went off in Olivia's head. Robert was the owner's son. Mr. Jenner probably felt that every move he made was reported to the head office. No wonder he was nervous and grouchy. She judged it was high time to get out of his way.

"I'll just go talk to him, then," Olivia said. She shut the door carefully behind her and hurried away.

"Did you find him?" Robert asked as she walked up to him at the tie counter.

Olivia let her breath out slowly. "Yeah. He's pretty . . . uh, I mean he's—"

"Paranoid?" Robert suggested. "I know. He thinks I'm spying on him."

"Well, what *are* you doing working in this department?" Olivia asked.

Robert realigned a few ties so their ends were at the same level and then shrugged. "I figure if I'm going to be running this business someday, I should know it from the ground up. I've been working in different departments, getting a feel for how they all work."

"That makes sense," Olivia said.

"Thanks." Robert bowed.

"Well, since your father is paying me to *work*, will you show me around and tell me what I'm supposed to do?"

"Sure," Robert said. "It's pretty self-explanatory. First, you should walk around the department and see how everything is laid out. When you're done, I'll show you how to use the cash register, how to write up credit card slips—"

"OK, but one thing at a time," Olivia begged. "I'll go scout around and come back for more instructions!"

Olivia walked away to tour the department. Robert seemed like a really nice guy. Of course, he was the private-school-and-tennis-lessons type of boy, with perfectly styled hair and a polished manner to go with his expensive clothes. He even wore cuff links!

But he was *nice* in spite of those serious drawbacks, Olivia told herself with a little smile.

Olivia wandered around the department, taking time to examine the sorts of clothing available and to acquaint herself with the layout.

"Miss Davidson," came a stern voice.

Olivia whirled around to face Mr. Jenner. "I've been getting to know the stock," she explained quickly. She saw the mistrust in his face and added, "Robert said it was what I should do first."

"Oh. Well, if Robert said so, it's OK." Mr. Jenner looked her up and down. "In the future, please try to dress more appropriately when you come to work in my department. A decent suit would do."

He turned and walked away.

"Yikes," Olivia muttered. She didn't own a "decent suit," and she thought she would probably feel faint if she did!

Olivia glanced across the department and caught Robert's eye. As soon as Mr. Jenner's back was turned, Robert pulled a very funny expression with his nose in the air and his eyes closed. Olivia clapped a hand over her mouth to cover a giggle.

Robert was preppy, conservative, and Establishment with a capital *E*. But he was also an ally, Olivia realized with pleasant surprise. An unlikely ally, but that was what he was, all the same. Working at Simpson's might actually be fun because of him.

Olivia wandered over to a Christmas display that could have been titled "Country Gentleman's Christmas." There was a fake fireplace with mantel, a leather armchair and ottoman, and a stack of fishing magazines on a side table. An empty brandy snifter sat next to the magazines. Clothes from the department were beautifully arranged in the setting.

"What do you think of it?" Robert asked as he joined her.

Olivia opened her mouth to say, "I hate it." But just in time she remembered that he *was* the boss's son, in spite of his casual attitude.

"It sure has that country squire look," she said diplomatically.

"You don't like it?"

"I didn't say that," Olivia said quickly. She imagined Robert might think it was the most tasteful display in the store.

"But you would do something different?" Robert said.

Olivia shrugged. "Well, we all have different tastes. This honestly isn't my taste, but that doesn't mean it isn't a good arrangement." She frowned at the display. "I do think it needs something to kick it up a little, though."

"Like what?" Robert asked.

"Well, I—" Olivia began.

"No, wait," he cut in. "Let me ask Jenner if we can change it first, and then you can go to it."

"OK, if you think he'll let us," Olivia agreed.

Robert grinned. "I can always pull rank, you know."

Within a few minutes, Robert returned with

permission for Olivia to change the display. "Just tell me what you need," he told her.

Olivia was excited by the challenge. Working on the display would be a lot more fun than selling men's shirts. She looked critically at the "Gentleman's Christmas."

"I'll need some thumbtacks and pins. And can I use some of the stuff in the department?" she asked hopefully.

Robert smiled. "You've got it. Use anything you want. I bet you'll do a great job."

"Thanks. This is going to be fun." Then Olivia hurried off to collect merchandise to add to the display. Soon she had her arms full, and she met Robert back by the fake fireplace. He handed her a pincushion and a box of pushpins.

"I have to go wait on someone. I'll see you later," he told her.

Olivia nodded and got to work. When she examined the mantelpiece, she found it was simply made of painted styrofoam. She opened up several packages of the most brightly colored striped and argyle socks she could find. She took one from each pair and hung them from the fireplace with the pushpins. Then she took the pair of black boots she had collected and attached them to the back of the fireplace so that they looked like the feet of Santa Claus coming down the chimney.

Then she stacked up the sweaters and shirts that had been part of the display, and tied them together with colored silk ties, making a big bow on top of each package. Into the brandy snifter she stuffed a burnt-orange pocket square and pulled the corners up and over the rim so that the effect was of brandy splashing over the side of the glass.

"Miss Davidson." Mr. Jenner's voice was like ice water.

Olivia turned slowly. "How do you like it, Mr. Jenner?"

"Miss Davidson, this is *not* the way we do things here at Simpson's," Mr. Jenner said with frigid dignity. "This is not a joke."

Olivia felt her heart sink. "I'm not trying to make a joke," she explained. "I'm only trying to bring some humor to the display."

"We do not—" Mr. Jenner began.

Just then Robert walked up. His face brightened when he saw Olivia's work. Olivia bit her lip. If she had Robert on her side, she was sure Mr. Jenner would let the display stay as it was. She waited.

"This is great," Robert said at last. "This is very creative."

"I was just saying the same thing," Mr. Jenner said. He looked at Olivia sourly. "*Very* creative."

"You really have a flair for decorating, Olivia," Robert said. "So, can we keep it like this, Mr. Jenner?"

Mr. Jenner gave Robert a wintry smile. "Of

course," he said. Then he turned on his heel and walked away.

"Now I have an enemy for life," Olivia groaned, slumping down on the armchair.

"Oh, forget about him," Robert said. "You've done a great job and he just doesn't want to admit it, that's all."

"And he doesn't want you to tell on him, either," Olivia pointed out with a trace of sarcasm.

Robert blushed. "I wish he would just get over that," he said.

"Well, thanks for sticking up for me."

"I bet you're an artistic person," Robert said. "Am I right?"

Olivia smiled, stood, and began to pick up the empty plastic wrappers. "Yeah, I'm artistic. I paint."

"You paint? Like pictures of things?" Robert asked. He laughed. "I can't even draw a straight line."

"I'm not very interested in pictures of things," Olivia said patiently. "Or in straight lines, either."

"I'd love to see your paintings," he said as he helped her clean up.

"No, you wouldn't," Olivia told him with a shake of her head.

"I mean it," Robert said. "I'm really interested."

Olivia looked at him doubtfully. If appearances meant anything, Robert would not like her abstract paintings. *But he might just surprise me*, she told herself.

"OK, sure," she agreed.

"Maybe this weekend?" Robert asked hopefully.

"Maybe," Olivia said with a laugh. "We'll see."

Eleven

Emily took the Sweet Valley exit off the highway and drove down the ramp. It was Friday and she was tired from a long day of driving and another campus tour and interview. Waiting for the red light to change, she glanced over at the folders on the seat next to her. Even with all the organizing she had done, she was still having trouble keeping everything straight in her head.

A car honked behind her. Startled, she looked up and saw that the light was green. She put the rental car into gear and started to drive again.

"Pay attention," she told herself. But her mind wandered back to the interview she had had that morning.

Suddenly, Emily realized she was driving in a part of town she was not at all familiar with. She frowned and began to search for a familiar landmark. After a few minutes she passed a furniture store that seemed vaguely familiar. And then she recognized the coffee shop Olivia had taken her to the other night. With a smile of relief, she pulled up to the curb and turned off the engine. She could do with a cup of coffee to go.

Emily walked into the coffee shop and glanced around. She wondered if James was there. She had no real reason to think he would be.

Then she saw him. He was sitting at a booth, scowling over a book. Emily ordered a container of coffee and took it over to his table.

"Hi," she said. "Remember me?"

James looked up in surprise. "Oh, Emily. What brings you here?"

"I got lost," Emily admitted, sitting down across from him. "When I saw this place I just stopped to get my bearings."

"Land ho," James said with a grin.

"Something like that," Emily agreed.

They smiled awkwardly. Emily was not sure what to talk to James about. She had never met anyone like him, but she found him interesting. She felt a desire to find out more about him.

"What are you reading?" she asked.

James closed the book. "It's about color theory," he explained.

Emily smiled, and James went on. "It talks about how colors affect people psychologically, and about the effects of different color combinations on people's emotions."

"May I see it?" Emily asked. James shoved the book across the table and Emily began to leaf through it. Page after page was covered with little squares of color: red with blue, red with orange, red with green, red with brown. It was like a crazy checkerboard. She shook her head. She didn't see the point.

"Is it like, red colors are warm and blue colors are cool?" she asked, looking up at James again.

He winced slightly. "Well, something like that. But reds can be cool, and blues can be warm, too."

"Really?" Emily flipped through more of the pages. "I didn't realize that."

"It's not something you'd really think about unless you were a painter," James said, taking the book back and closing it firmly. "I guess it's probably pretty boring to you."

"Of course it isn't," Emily said quickly. "I'm very interested in art."

James smiled. "You're just being polite."

"No. Honest," Emily protested, and then she realized how she must look to James. Like a contestant in a law school fashion show. Even Emily knew that her green kilt, white blouse, and blue flats didn't exactly qualify as arty.

Emily smiled nervously. *Maybe if he saw me in something different*, she thought, *he would find me more exciting to talk to.* Emily smiled again and took a sip of her coffee. She really did wish he would open up to her. James Yates was definitely the most intriguing guy Emily had ever met.

Olivia slept late on Saturday. When she finally opened her eyes to peek across the room, she was relieved to see Emily's bed empty—and already made. Olivia knew her cousin and Aunt June had planned an early start to their drive up the coast. There would be no pressure on Olivia to entertain Emily that day.

Oliva rolled over and got out of bed. She had part of the morning and afternoon ahead of her. At four o'clock she had to report to Simpson's for the evening shift, but she had plenty of time before that to get some painting done. Olivia put on a pair of blue gauze overalls over a red tank top and padded downstairs in her bare feet.

As she passed the door out to the patio, she overheard her Aunt June's voice. It was obvious that Emily and her mother hadn't left quite yet.

"For a while there, I thought you might actually go through with it," Aunt June said with a laugh. "You had me pretty worried."

"Yes, well, I was young," Olivia's mother replied.

"And thank *goodness* you grew out of it," Aunt June went on. "Can you imagine what your life would have been like? It's just ridiculous even thinking about it now."

There was a pause. Then Mrs. Davidson said, "It's not that ridiculous, June. It was never *ridiculous*."

Olivia frowned and walked on past the door. She hated to admit that she didn't really like her Aunt June very much. There was something very hard about her. And it was pretty clear to Olivia that her mother didn't always feel that comfortable around her, either. Olivia was secretly glad that Aunt June would be leaving tomorrow.

"Well, you decided to join us, I see," Mr. Davidson said as Olivia walked into the kitchen. "There's a little bit of coffee left."

"I can make another pot," Emily offered, looking up from one of her color-coded college files.

"No, thanks," Olivia said as she grabbed a glass of orange juice. "I'm just going out to my studio to work. I'll see you all later."

Olivia went out to the garage and rolled the overhead door up to let in the morning light.

Then she sat on a stool and examined her "Mother and Child" painting for several minutes.

It still filled her with intense feelings, and that was a good sign. It meant that the picture had truly absorbed those emotions, rather than just having reflected them for a few moments in time. Olivia nodded, set down her empty juice glass, and started back to work.

"Bye, Olivia!" Emily called out a few minutes later.

Olivia looked up from mixing colors on her palette to wave goodbye. Through the open garage door she could see her cousin and aunt getting into the rental car.

"Have a good day!" Olivia called.

She watched them drive away, and then turned her attention to her paints again. Once she had mixed a good amount of the color she wanted, she picked up a wide brush and saturated it with paint. Then she faced her easel, pushed her hair back from her face, and began painting in wide, circular strokes. Within moments, she was totally oblivious to the rest of the world.

Finally, the sound of a car door slamming behind her brought her back to earth. And then she heard her name called.

"Olivia?"

She turned around in surprise. It was Robert Simpson. Because she was still half-immersed in her painting, she didn't speak immediately. Robert walked slowly toward the garage door.

"Olivia?" he repeated doubtfully.

"Oh, hi, Robert," she said now. She smiled. "Come on in."

"I wasn't sure it was you," Robert said as he walked into the garage. He was dressed for tennis, with a navy-blue polo shirt and bright white shorts and sneakers. A pair of sunglasses sat on top of his head.

"I didn't think you'd really come," Olivia said. "I didn't even know you knew where I lived."

"Well, finding out your address was easy. And I really wanted to see your paintings," he explained with a smile. "I guess this is the real you, huh?" Robert added with a nod at her outfit.

Olivia glanced down at herself and laughed. In her three days of working at Simpson's she had worn almost her entire wardrobe of somewhat "normal" clothes. Robert must have assumed she was actually a "normal" person. "This is the real me. Do I look like a bag lady or like someone who just escaped from a lunatic asylum?"

"No," he said quickly. "I didn't mean—"

"I'm crazy, but not dangerous," Olivia assured him.

Robert looked a little bit embarrassed. "Well, uh . . . so, can I see your stuff?" he asked.

"Sure. This is what I'm working on now," Olivia said excitedly, pointing to her easel. "How do you like it? It's called 'Mother and Child.' "

Robert stood in front of the picture. His face wore a solemn frown. The silence stretched out.

"When are you going to put in the mother and child?" he finally asked.

Olivia felt her heart make a little bump inside her chest. Robert's response to her painting was exactly what she should have expected. But still, it hurt.

"It's pretty much finished," she said quietly. "It's supposed to evoke the emotions of a mother with her child."

"Oh." Robert looked at her, and then back at the picture. "Is that what they call abstract?" he asked with a puzzled smile.

"That's right," Olivia said. For some reason, she felt embarrassed. If she tried to look at the painting through Robert's eyes, what she probably would see was a wild swirl of colors, a large round blob with a smaller round blob inside of it. *Does it really mean anything at all?* she wondered with a spasm of doubt. She turned away and began to fuss with some brushes and tubes of paint.

"I don't really understand modern art, I guess," Robert admitted. "If it's not a picture *of* something, then what is it?"

120

Olivia shrugged uncomfortably and bent over her workbench to scrape her palette clean. "It's a picture of something *inside*."

While she worked she could hear Robert walking around the garage, stopping now and then to look at the pictures on the walls.

"Hey," Robert said. "This is really nice."

Olivia glanced over her shoulder. Robert was standing in front of a picture she had done as a sort of experiment. It was a seascape, with the sky, the ocean, and the beach represented by long horizontal bands of blue, green, and tan. The only other spot of color was a white triangle, representing a sailboat, cutting across the green.

"I like this," Robert said with admiration. "It really looks like the beach. You did this really well."

There was no missing the appreciation in his voice: Robert was truly impressed. The only problem was that he was impressed by a picture that didn't interest *her* at all.

"Do you have any others like this?" Robert asked eagerly.

Olivia licked her lips and glanced nervously around her studio. "Well, sort of," she said.

"Can I see them?" Robert asked.

With a sinking, sad feeling, Olivia walked to the metal cabinet that housed her rejects. Inside were stored several canvases similar to her beach scene: still lifes with vases of flowers and piles of fruit, a picture with lines of palm trees marching into the distance, one of a swimming pool reflecting a diver.

"You paint so well," Robert said as he looked through them. He smiled at her warmly. "I think your work is really good."

"Thanks," Olivia replied in a dull voice.

"Thanks for showing me your pictures," Robert said, oblivious to Olivia's discomfort.

"You're welcome." Olivia nervously pleated the thin material of her overalls.

"Well, I have to go now. Are you working later today?" Robert asked as he headed for the door.

Olivia nodded.

"I'll see you later, then." Robert walked out to his car. Then he lifted his hand in a wave, got in, and drove away.

Olivia sat down on her workbench and hung her head. Robert's visit had turned her upside down, somehow. In the brief moment she had tried to see her work through his eyes, she had seen something she didn't like, something she couldn't appreciate. Though Robert had been nothing but polite, his visit had left her feeling like a kid playing dress-up, messing around with paints and calling it art. *Who am I kidding but myself?* she wondered.

Olivia knew that Robert wasn't an expert on painting. But *most* people weren't. Could she afford to ignore their reactions to her work? If she ever expected to make a living as a painter, she could not just paint what she wanted and forget about painting what the public wanted to see.

Olivia took a deep breath and squared her shoulders. If she was really going to start being practical about her life, if she truly wanted to start planning for her future, she would have to start thinking about painting for the public.

"And the public won't want to buy this," Olivia muttered, glaring at her "Mother and Child."

It was still wet, but Olivia didn't care. She took the painting off the easel and stuck it in the cabinet.

Twelve

Jessica reported for work on Wednesday with a grim sense of determination. She was going to meet Robert Simpson that afternoon or she was going to quit. But she had no idea of how she was actually going to manage to meet him. She mulled over the problem while she restocked a rack with teddy-bear-print sleep sets. As she leaned over to take some pieces out of the carton, her name tag snagged on a little T-shirt.

"That's it," she exclaimed. She straightened up quickly and hurried over to the cash register desk.

"Excuse me, Mrs. Crawshaw," she said as she reached for the store telephone and the department directory. She leafed through the pages until she found Mrs. Endicott's number in the personnel office.

"Mrs. Endicott speaking," came the familiar husky voice.

"Hi, this is Jessica Wakefield," Jessica said brightly. "I just found Robert Simpson's ID card. He must have dropped it. If you tell me where he's working today, I could just run over to the department and return it to him."

"Oh, that's very nice of you, Jessica," Mrs. Endicott said. "Let's see, I think he must still be in the menswear department. Fourth floor."

Jessica made a fist and said, *"Yes!"* under her breath.

"Excuse me?" Mrs. Endicott asked politely.

"I said, yes, I know what floor it's on," Jessica explained in her sweetest voice. "Thanks."

She hung up the telephone and looked imploringly at Mrs. Crawshaw. "Can I do a teensy-tiny errand that will only take about three seconds?"

"Certainly, Jessica," Mrs. Crawshaw said. "Say hello to Robert for me."

"Sure," Jessica replied. She slipped out from behind the desk and tried not to race too wildly out of the infants' and children's department.

On the escalator, Jessica wondered if she could concoct some sort of story that would get her transferred to the menswear department. But she would wait and see if Robert was everything he was cracked up to be before she went to that trouble.

The closer she came to the fourth floor, the more impatient she became. Finally, Jessica pushed her way past a lady holding three shopping bags and jumped off the last steps. Hurriedly, she crossed the marble floor. The perfectly coiffed male mannequins of the menswear department were straight ahead.

This is it, she thought happily, slowing her pace to a moderate rush.

When she reached the department, Jessica took a quick, appraising look around. Standing at the wallets counter was Olivia Davidson, wearing a plain blue dress. *That's strange,* Jessica thought. But then her attention was caught by the adorable, well-dressed boy who was talking to Olivia. It had to be Robert Simpson.

Putting on her most charming smile, Jessica walked over to the counter and fixed her eyes on Olivia.

"I didn't know you were working here, Olivia!" she exclaimed. "You never even told me!"

"I—I guess I forgot to mention it to you, Jessica," Olivia said, confused.

"You're *so* forgetful," Jessica responded playfully. And then she turned and flashed a smile at Robert. "Hi. I'm Jessica Wakefield—infants and children."

Robert Simpson had a very beguiling way of

tilting his head. He was even cuter than Lila had reported, Jessica noted.

"Hi. I'm Robert Simpson."

"Any relation to our boss?" Jessica asked innocently as she leaned on the counter, her back to Olivia.

"He's my father," Robert admitted.

"You're kidding me!" Jessica squealed. "I meant it as a joke. I didn't even know he had a son!"

"Well, he does and it's me," Robert said, looking at Olivia with a sheepish grin.

"Robert, maybe you can give me some advice," Jessica said, continuing not to look at Olivia and effectively cutting her out of the conversation. "I need to pick out a wallet—not for a boyfriend or anything. For my father."

Robert nodded. "Sure. We've got some really nice ones here," he said, sliding open the back of the cabinet they were standing by.

"Oh, I was hoping you could show me the ones down at the *other* end," Jessica said.

"No problem." Robert followed her away from Olivia and opened the case. He took out several wallets for her to look at and said, "Take your time. If you have any questions, let me know."

Then he walked back to the other end of the counter and resumed his conversation with Olivia.

Jessica scowled, picked up the first wallet, and acted out the part of a careful customer.

She opened every flap and examined each slot, but she paid no attention to it at all. Her attention was directed toward overhearing Robert and Olivia's conversation.

"I want to ask you something, Olivia," Robert said. "Some friends of mine are having a party on Saturday night. Would you like to go with me?"

Jessica took a small step closer, still keeping her eyes on the wallet and her ears pricked.

"I'm sorry," Olivia said. "I already have plans."

But I don't! Jessica wanted to shout out.

"Gee, Robert?" Jessica said in a winsome tone.

Robert walked back to where she stood. "Find something you like?" he asked.

"Well, I just can't make up my mind." Jessica held out two different wallets. "Which one of these do *you* like best?" She looked at him seductively.

"I like them both," Robert answered with a friendly smile. "But I *have* to say that," he teased.

"You're a rat," Jessica said in a voice that really said, "You're adorable."

Robert started to put the wallets back in the glass case. "Why don't you think about it and then come back?" He glanced at Olivia again, and then back to Jessica. "It was nice meeting you."

No matter how she looked at it, Jessica could not deny that she was getting the brush-off.

And in favor of Olivia Davidson, too. It was enough to make her question Robert's sanity. But then he tilted his head again as he reached up for the last of the wallets, and Jessica's knees turned to water.

Sane or not, Robert was irresistable. Getting him interested in her was just going to be more of a challenge than she had anticipated. No problem.

"It was nice meeting you, too," Jessica said sweetly.

Step one was accomplished. She had met Robert Simpson. Now it was time to start planning step two.

Emily poured herself a glass of iced tea and sat at the kitchen table. She had planned her itinerary so that she had one day off to rest and review her notes.

The only problem was that she didn't *feel* like reviewing her notes. While she sat meditatively chewing an ice cube, she began to think about James.

She didn't know what it was about him that intrigued her. What she did know was that when she thought of James, she began to question her own mania for making lists and schedules. Being unorganized was a kind of anarchy, she thought. It was scary, but it was also attractive in its own way.

Without stopping to analyze what she was doing, Emily went upstairs and opened Olivia's closet. She touched the soft fabric of a black, high-waisted jumper. Then she slipped it off its hanger and held it up against herself. The change was startling, and Emily liked it. She quickly pulled one of Olivia's batik T-shirts out of a drawer and changed into the new outfit. Emily turned from side to side, letting the long skirt of the jumper swing back and forth around her legs.

Then she took the navy-and-pink striped headband from her hair and tossed it onto her bed. She went downstairs, left the house, and headed downtown in the rental car.

By the time she got to the coffee shop, Emily was already regretting her impulsiveness. She sat in the car by the curb, shaking her head slowly.

What a dumb thing to do. He probably isn't even here, she scolded herself.

Emily was embarrassed by what she had done. She felt ridiculous in her cousin's clothes. She knew she was just trying to impress James, trying to show him she was more artistic than he gave her credit for, than she really was.

With a sigh, Emily leaned her head back against the headrest and gazed out the windshield. Then she saw James crossing the street, his portfolio under his arm.

Emily realized that he hadn't noticed her yet. She tried to duck down in the seat, but it was too late. James stopped, squinted, and then came toward her.

"Emily?" he asked.

Emily smiled weakly. "Hi, James."

"Did you get lost again?" James asked as he rested his portfolio on the roof of the car.

"No, I was just—" Emily broke off. It wasn't often that she was at a loss for words. "I just thought I would stop by and say hello," she finally confessed.

"Oh. Well, hi. I'm on my way home. Want to come up and have a soda or something? My apartment is just down the block."

Emily could tell it was no more than a friendly invitation. But she wanted to see his place, anyway. "Sure," she said, opening the door.

She half expected him to make some comment about the way she was dressed, but he didn't. He swung his portfolio off the roof of the car and led the way.

"Some of the universities I've been interviewing at have really fantastic art departments," Emily began as she fell into step beside him.

"Did you take a look at any of them?" James asked.

Emily shook her head. "Well, not exactly. But

the *brochures* say they have really fantastic art departments." Emily cursed herself silently. She knew she sounded like an idiot.

"This is it," James said finally. He led the way up the narrow stairs to the apartment over the television repair shop. "If we're lucky, I'll actually have a can of soda left."

"It doesn't matter," Emily put in hastily.

James opened the door. "That's a relief. Because I probably don't have any."

Emily laughed. She really liked James. He said exactly what he was thinking, and didn't try to cover himself with automatic social phrases. It was nice to meet someone whose behavior she couldn't predict.

But as she followed James into his apartment, Emily felt her stomach swoop. She had never been in such a depressing place. It was the strongest argument she had ever encountered for getting a degree in business. Emily knew immediately that she could never live like that.

"So, this is your home?" she asked, trying not to sound critical or disappointed.

"For now it is," James said. "Basically, my home is wherever I am. And wherever my work is. I could walk out of here today and never miss it."

Emily nodded. "I can believe that."

"But not because it's a dump," James said as he popped open a can of soda. "Want some?"

"No, thanks." Emily looked around for a clean place to sit and found none.

"So, did you and Olivia grow up together?" James asked as he perched on the window sill.

Emily shook her head. "I live in Connecticut." She stared moodily at the palm of her hand for a moment, and then decided to take the plunge. "Olivia and I don't talk very much. I don't even know if you two are going out together or anything like that."

"No. It's nothing like that," James said simply. "Olivia's great and I think she's got a lot of talent. But I don't believe in all that relationship stuff. I don't even know what people mean when they talk about love."

A warm flush spread across Emily's cheeks. "Well," she began. "I mean, you've been in love, haven't you?"

"No, I don't think so," James said. "I'm not even sure whether love is real or if it's just something our culture made up. Why? Have you ever been in love?" he asked, looking at her steadily.

Emily felt even more awkward. She shook her head.

"No, I haven't," she said shyly. "Not really."

She raised her eyes to look at him but James was gazing out the window. Now that Emily knew that he and Olivia were just friends, she realized what she had tried to deny before this moment. She liked James a lot, and she desperately wanted him to feel the same way about her.

Thirteen

After dinner on Thursday, Olivia swung up onto the kitchen counter, reached for the telephone, and dialed James's number. She twirled the cord around her index finger while she waited for him to answer.

"What?" came his distracted voice.

Olivia smiled. "It's me, Olivia," she said. "You sound busy."

"Oh, sorry." James sighed. "I'm working."

"So what else is new?" Olivia asked.

He laughed shortly. "Right. So what's up? Why weren't you in class last night?"

Olivia stared at her fingernails, feeling suddenly defensive and embarrassed. "Oh, well, I had to work yesterday afternoon. See, I started this part-time job, and I was so tired by the time I got home that I couldn't face the idea of going out again."

"I know how it is," James replied.

Olivia nodded. She had felt pretty ashamed of herself for having missed the class. But she *had* been exhausted. And she hadn't really felt up to dealing in intense, artistic terms after an afternoon at Simpson's.

"Anyway," she went on brightly, "you said you wanted to see that Buñuel film this weekend. Are we still on for Saturday night?"

"Saturday?" James repeated.

Olivia swallowed hard and waited for him to go on.

"Olivia, I'm really sorry," he said. "I'm trying to finish this painting by Monday morning. I can't take time out."

Olivia drew a deep breath to help fight down the disappointment she felt inside.

"I understand," she said. "The movie will be around for a couple of weeks. We can see it some other time."

"Right, some other time," James said gratefully. "Thanks for not being hurt."

Olivia closed her eyes. "Hurt?" she echoed. "Why would I be hurt?"

"Listen, I'll let you know when I finish the painting," James said. "I want you to see it."

"That'll be great," Olivia said. "I want to see it. Good luck."

"Thanks. Bye."

James hung up, and Olivia sat listening to the dial tone. She tried to tell herself that she really *wasn't* hurt. What difference did it make if she didn't see James on Saturday night? They didn't have that kind of obsessive, possessive friendship. And if she couldn't understand his need to paint, then she shouldn't be his friend at all, she told herself.

Olivia sighed, hung up the phone, and began to swing her legs back and forth.

"Hi," Emily said as she walked into the kitchen a few minutes later.

Olivia smiled faintly. "Hey."

"Is something wrong?" Emily asked, looking at Olivia over her shoulder as she poured herself a glass of water. "You look sort of down."

"Not really," Olivia said, hopping down from her perch. "I just feel like a dope right now. Would you believe I turned down a date for Saturday night because I thought I already had one? And now I don't."

She tried to laugh, and hoped she sounded like any other high school girl worrying about dates and boyfriends.

"Bummer," Emily said with a sympathetic smile. "Who did you turn down?"

Olivia rolled her eyes. "Robert Simpson. My boss's son, can you believe it? Mr. Corporation asked me to go to a party with him."

"Why don't you ask him if the invitation is still valid?" Emily asked her.

"I couldn't do that," Olivia said, shaking her head quickly.

"Why not? Go ahead and call him," Emily suggested.

Olivia folded her arms. Going to a party with Robert didn't quite compensate for missing the Buñuel film with James. But why should it have to compensate? she asked herself. Robert was a perfectly nice guy, even if he was very different from James.

"Yeah, why not?" she said to her cousin. "Why not?"

Emily grinned. "Go for it. I'll get out of your way."

Olivia smiled affectionately as her cousin left the room. Emily was really very sweet and thoughtful. Still smiling, she picked up the phone book and looked up the Simpsons' number.

"Hi, can I speak to Robert?" she asked when a woman answered the telephone.

"May I ask who is calling, please?" the woman replied in a stiff, formal voice.

"Olivia Davidson," Olivia said meekly. She tried to picture Robert's mother, but all she could see was a caricature of a queen in a tiara and expensive tennis clothes. She held one hand over the mouthpiece and giggled.

"Olivia? Hi," Robert said.

"Hi, Robert," Olivia said. Her humorous mental image of Mrs. Simpson had cheered her up so much that she felt as if she could say anything. She almost hoped she would shock Robert. "I'm calling to ask your forgiveness very humbly."

"What for?" he asked.

"I'm a jerk, that's why," Olivia told him. "I turned you down for that party because I had other plans, but now they're canceled and I'm hoping it's not too late to go with you. I'd rather die than stay home alone on a Saturday night," Olivia said with an extravagant sweep of her arm.

There was a pause. Then Robert said, "Well, sure. I wouldn't want you to die."

"I appreciate that," Olivia laughed.

"I have to tell you, though," Robert went on, "this is a bunch of people I know from the country club."

Olivia smiled. "Are you trying to tell me not to wear a Polynesian sarong and a tie-dyed coat?"

"No, no," Robert blustered. "I mean, it's just that you seem to—I mean—"

"Don't worry," Olivia said. "I'll try not to be *too* weird."

"Oh, fine. Whatever," Robert said, sounding very relieved. "I'll see you tomorrow at work."

After Olivia hung up the phone, the smile faded from her face. It was one thing to *sound* breezily confident. But she wasn't so sure she actually *felt* that way. She tried to imagine what Robert's friends would be like. They couldn't be that bad, she decided. Just because they went to prep schools and country clubs didn't mean she wouldn't be able to talk to them.

She really would have to find something appropriate to wear, though. Olivia usually saw parties as theatrical events. She actually *had* worn a sarong and a tie-dyed coat to the last party she had attended.

Olivia headed upstairs to her room. Emily was sitting in bed, reading *Business Week*.

"Did you call him?" Emily asked.

Olivia nodded absently. "I'm going to the party. Oh, I should have asked if you wanted to go, too! I'm sure it would be all right."

"No, thanks," Emily said as she flipped through a few pages of the magazine. "I'll find something else to do. I'm not big on parties, anyway."

"You're sure?" Olivia asked, suddenly hoping that Emily would change her mind. It might help to have someone along who would fit in better than she would.

"Yeah, I'm sure. What are you going to wear?" Emily asked.

Olivia flung herself onto her bed. "I have no idea. I think I'll have to get something new," she muttered.

"You could get something at Simpson's," Emily pointed out. "You could use your store discount. They have some really nice party dresses."

Olivia tried not to wince. She could see the dresses in her mind: drop-waisted dresses with velvet collars, tartan taffeta, and lace insets. That sort of dress just wouldn't be *her*. But it would be right for Robert's party.

"You could pick something out tomorrow when you're at work," Emily went on hopefully.

Olivia rolled over and hugged her pillow. "You're right," she said. "That's what I'll do."

By the time Olivia got to work on Friday afternoon, she had made up her mind. If she was going to make changes in her lifestyle, she would make changes in her image, too. It was time to grow up and stop acting like a little girl let loose in a costume shop.

"Olivia, hi," Robert said when he saw her.

"Hi." Olivia looked at him nervously for a moment. "Can I ask you for some advice?"

He smiled. "Sure."

"I was hoping you would help me pick out something for the party tomorrow night," she said. "I figured you would know what was suitable. I mean, you know your friends and I don't."

Olivia waited. Part of her was hoping that Robert would argue with her and say she should wear whatever she wanted to. But he didn't.

"You really want me to help you?" he asked with a beaming smile.

Olivia nodded. "Yes. If you don't mind."

"I don't mind at all! In fact, I saw something the other day that I thought would be perfect on you."

"Really?" Olivia asked, somewhat surprised. Robert was taking the task very seriously.

"I'll show it to you," Robert continued. "Hang on a second. Just let me get Mr. Jenner's permission for us to take a quick break."

In a few minutes Robert returned, and together they went to the Better Dresses section. *I was right to ask for his help*, Olivia told herself. He was bound to pick out the right kind of dress.

"This is it," Robert said as he took a dark green velvet dress off a rack. The dress had long sleeves, a tight waist, a straight skirt, and an off-white lace collar and cuffs. "Do you like it?"

"It's a nice color," Olivia said. She fingered the soft velvet. She would never have picked it out for herself, but maybe Robert was right. Maybe it would be perfect for her.

"Try it on," he urged.

Olivia found a dress in her size and headed for the dressing room. She tugged it down over her head and zipped it up. Without a glance in the mirror, she walked right outside to show Robert.

His face lit up when he saw her. "I knew it! It looks great on you. You look very sophisticated and glamorous, Olivia."

She laughed. "Oh, be serious."

"I am," Robert said. "It's really perfect. Do you like it?"

"I guess so," Olivia said, holding out her arm to look at the lacy cuff.

Robert looked delighted. "You should buy it. And I'm not just saying that because it's my dad's store, you know!"

"I know," Olivia said. She could tell that Robert really liked the way she looked in the dress. It was hard not to feel somewhat flattered.

"Are you sure it's the right kind of thing to wear to this party?" she asked. "Isn't it a little dressy?"

He shook his head emphatically. "It's perfect!"

"OK," Olivia agreed. "If you say so."

Olivia went back to the dressing room and took a long look at herself in the mirror. She thought she looked like a different person. Robert's words came back to her: sophisticated, glamorous. By that did he mean that she usually looked juvenile and silly? Maybe he did, and maybe he was right.

Olivia gave her reflection a decisive nod. She was going to go to that party in this dress, and she was going to have a great time.

Emily parked the car down the street from James's apartment on Saturday afternoon. She knew she was taking a risk by dropping in without warning. But she felt like taking risks for once in her life. Maybe it was being away from home. And wearing another of Olivia's outfits also gave her a kind of borrowed courage. Out in southern California, wearing blue leggings and a long checked sweater, she didn't feel so much like the old Emily.

The steep stairway of his building echoed with her footsteps, almost drowning out the sound of her heart knocking against her ribs.

I've never done this before, Emily told herself over and over. *I cannot believe I'm doing this.*

When she finally stood facing his door, she hesitated. And then she knocked.

"Hi, I know I'm barging in," she said quickly, before James had fully opened the door.

James looked at her with obvious surprise. "That's OK. I was just taking a break. Come on in."

Emily followed him into the dingy apartment and once again felt as if she were entering a new world.

"Want some tea?" James asked. "It takes a long time for the kettle to boil, but it will, eventually."

Emily shook her head nervously. "No, that's OK." She looked around. The area by James's easel was littered with paint tubes and crumpled rags. "Are you working?"

"Yes," he replied, fiddling with the stove. "I'm in one of my frenzies. When I get like this all I can do is paint. I can't take time for anything else. I even had to cancel plans with Olivia. We were supposed to see a movie tonight."

Emily could hear the intensity in his voice. He was so wrapped up in his work, he probably wasn't even curious about her dropping in. She could almost believe he would forget she was there if she didn't say anything.

"When you see her, tell her again that I'm sorry, OK?" James added.

"Sure. But I wouldn't worry about her," Emily said. "She's going to a party tonight."

"Good," James replied with a smile. "Are you going with her?"

Emily shook her head. "She's going with her boss's son, Robert Simpson."

"You mean, like a date?" James asked. He looked directly at her for a moment, and then turned back to the stove.

"I guess it's like a date," Emily said uncertainly.

James nodded, his back still to her. "Oh."

"He's a really nice guy, according to Olivia," Emily went on. "He's going into the family business—you know, Simpson's department store—and he's working in Olivia's department. That's how they met. He even helped her pick out a new dress for this party. It's very pretty."

James nodded and opened a cupboard.

Emily watched him rummage through it. He seemed edgy all of a sudden. If she didn't know how he felt about relationships, Emily might have thought he was upset about Olivia going out with Robert. But according to Olivia, James had been very emphatic about not making any personal commitments. He was probably still preoccupied with his work, that was all. Emily began to worry again that she was intruding.

"Listen, I should go," she said awkwardly.

"Well, thanks for stopping by," James said, hardly glancing at her as he played with a small box of tea bags.

Emily took a few steps toward the door. And then she stopped. She couldn't leave without finding out if she had made a mistake.

"You're not upset about Olivia going out with Robert, are you?" she asked.

James looked at her with an expression of amazement. "No, of course not."

"Oh. OK." Emily smiled. "Well, I'll see you around."

"Bye," James said as he turned and walked toward his easel. Emily closed the apartment door behind her. Knowing how James felt about honesty, Emily was sure he was telling the truth. He really didn't care if Olivia went out with Robert Simpson. And there was no reason why Emily shouldn't have mentioned it.

Fourteen

Olivia opened her closet. Her new green dress was on a hanger, the tags and a card of extra green velvet buttons still attached. Reluctantly, she pulled the dress out, cut off the tags, and put it on. As she regarded her reflection she could not help but see the dress as unimaginative. There had to be something she could add to it that would give it some character. If she had something green or red . . .

Olivia immediately thought of the holly wreath hanging on their front door. She ran downstairs, opened the door, and broke off a sprig of shiny green leaves and bright red berries. When she stepped back inside again, she stood in front of the hall mirror and tucked the holly sprig behind one ear. The leaves matched her dress perfectly, and the berries added just the right note of brightness.

"Plus, it befits the season," she told herself happily.

Olivia ran back upstairs to finish dressing.

"You look so pretty," Mrs. Davidson said, coming into Olivia's room a few minutes later.

"Thanks, Mom," Olivia said as she adjusted the holly sprig to a jauntier angle.

Mrs. Davidson was beaming. "And I know I shouldn't say this," Olivia's mother continued, "but I'm so thrilled that you're going out with Robert. He's such a nice boy."

"Yes, he is," Olivia agreed. But for some reason, she felt a little sad admitting it. *This is all it takes to please my mother*, she realized. *I guess I've always disappointed her before.*

"Now hurry up. Robert will be here any minute," Mrs. Davidson said cheerfully. "Have a wonderful time, sweetheart."

Olivia nodded. "I'll try."

When Robert arrived a few minutes later, Olivia was downstairs and ready. She gave her reflection one last critical glance, drew a deep breath, and answered the door.

"Hi," she said.

Robert smiled. His eyes went briefly to the holly tucked behind her ear, but he didn't say anything about it. "Hi. You look nice."

Olivia felt a strange, twisting sensation inside. Just by putting on a modest, conservative dress, she was getting compliments. Ordinarily, people didn't mention her appearance unless it was to comment on how outrageous she looked. But now, two people—her mother and Robert—had responded very positively. It was hard to know what to think of it.

"Let's go," she said. "So, tell me about the people at this party."

"They're a great bunch," Robert replied earnestly as they headed for his car. "I know you'll like them. My best friend will be there, the guy I've gone to tennis and sailing camp with since we were six years old."

Olivia nodded. "What's he like?"

"Tim's great. His father runs an executive search firm." Robert turned the car onto the coast highway. "Tim's planning to get into that, too, but first he's going to go to law school."

"Law school? Doesn't he have to go to college first?" Olivia asked.

"Oh, sure. He's been accepted early admission to Princeton," Robert told her nonchalantly. "He'll probably go out for the tennis team, too."

Olivia tried to imagine herself talking to Tim about sailing and tennis and law school and executive headhunters. She couldn't see it. Suddenly she wished she had taken the tennis lessons her parents had offered, or that she knew something about how the stock market worked. She was suddenly afraid that she would look like an ignoramus in front of Robert's friends.

"Who else will be there?" she asked quietly.

"Well, some people I know through my family," Robert went on pleasantly. "People whose parents socialize with my parents or who know them through political connections, that sort of thing."

Great! Olivia told herself gloomily. Then she gave herself a mental shake. Just because they played tennis or went to prep school or participated in political organizations didn't mean that they were stuffy or narrow-minded. Right now, *she* was the narrow-minded one. Her own lack of understanding was making her put up barriers.

"This is it," Robert said as they headed up a long, sweeping driveway. At the top of the driveway stood an imposing mansion overlooking the Pacific Ocean. The sun was setting, lighting the cliffs with a golden glow. The spectacular beauty of the site took Olivia's breath away.

But the house was a different matter. It was very grand, but to Olivia, it looked cold. *Too many plate-glass windows*, she thought. *Somebody paid a lot of money to a very expensive architect.*

Robert switched off the ignition and turned to Olivia. "Nice, isn't it?"

She nodded. "Mmm. Yes."

"Come on, don't be nervous," he said gently. "You'll like my friends."

Olivia smiled and followed Robert to the door. Inside, a crowd of high school and college students were standing around talking; others were relaxing on luxurious leather couches. Rock music was playing softly on the stereo. Olivia immediately made note of the clothes the other girls were wearing. She was no expert on expensive designer outfits, but she could tell that the dresses in the room represented an awful lot of money.

"Olivia, this is Chas, Laura, Brandon, Chris, Heather, and another Brandon," Robert said, pointing out face after well-groomed face.

Olivia felt so ill at ease that the names went right out of her head as soon as she heard them. She just smiled nervously and nodded.

"I'll get you something to drink," Robert said. "I'll be right back."

"Sure," Olivia said quickly. She looked around, almost in a panic now. Three elegant girls sitting on a nearby sofa smiled at her and made room for her to join them. Olivia lowered herself to the edge of the seat and smoothed the velvet dress over her knees.

"Hi," she said.

"You came with Robert Simpson?" one of them asked.

Olivia nodded. "My name is Olivia," she said.

"So, where did you apply?" another of the girls asked the girl across from Olivia.

"Swarthmore, Georgetown, and Oberlin," she replied, lightly tossing her straight blond hair. "The essays were such a bore!"

"Those are the colleges you applied to?" Olivia asked. She tried desperately to remember some of the college application trivia she had heard from Emily. "The deadline is usually early January, right?"

The first girl let out a lazy laugh. "Well, sure, but I had mine done by Thanksgiving break. College admissions offices pay attention when an application comes in early, you know."

"Oh, really?" Olivia said nervously.

"Where did you apply, Olivia?" one of the others asked. This one had red hair and Olivia thought she remembered Robert saying her name was Margot. Still, she was afraid to take a chance on calling her anything, just in case she was wrong.

"What are your schools?" the first one asked again.

"Me? Oh, I'm still a junior. I haven't even started looking at colleges yet."

The first girl stared at her. "You haven't started looking? Gosh, I've known since about seventh grade where I wanted to go to college—the University of Virginia, where my father went. I even know which dorm I want to live in."

"Well, I'm not even sure I'm going to go to college, actually," Olivia added recklessly.

"What kind of a career do you want to have?" the redheaded girl asked.

Olivia felt the sprig of holly in her hair starting to slip. She shoved it back into place. "I want to be a painter."

"A painter?" The red-haired girl arched her eyebrows skeptically. "But how are you going to support yourself?"

"Maybe she's going to marry a rich husband, Margot," the third girl suggested with a dry laugh.

"She wouldn't need to if she had your trust fund, Diana," Margot said.

Olivia tried to smile. "Well, I don't really think in terms of a *career*," she explained. "Painting is just what I feel I have to do."

"You could go into architecture," Diana offered.

"Or advertising," Margot said. "There's a lot of money in advertising."

The first girl, the blond one, nodded eagerly. "I thought about advertising for a while. But what I really want to do is run a nanny service."

"Come on, Beryl!" Margot laughed.

"I'm serious," Beryl insisted. "My mother had so much trouble getting good nannies when I was little. There are so many *hassles* with foreign girls. The immigration headaches are unbelievable, and half of them don't even know English. It's ridiculous."

153

Olivia looked from one girl to the other. She had nothing at all to contribute to the conversation. She didn't know anything about nannies or careers in advertising and architecture or choosing a college. She felt like an idiot. These girls, only a year older than she, seemed to have their entire lives mapped out. Olivia felt very inadequate, like a little girl at a grown-up party.

"So, Olivia, what kind of paintings do you do?" Diana asked her.

"Well . . ." Olivia licked her lips. "I'm pretty much into abstract paintings," she said.

"That's the only kind *I* can do," Beryl said with a giggle. "Just like finger painting. A bunch of swirls—that's the extent of my creative genius."

The others laughed. Olivia felt her face turn pink. Her work *did* sound childish, put that way. She knew her painting was important. But she also knew that she couldn't seem to make other people understand why. And to be honest, lately she couldn't always seem to make *herself* understand why.

"You know, animators make a ton of money," Margot said. "Today, a lot of animation is computerized. You know, Olivia, you could—"

Olivia stood up abruptly, her face flaming with embarrassment. "Sorry. I see Robert. I have to tell him something."

The trio of girls stared at her in surprise. Olivia knew they were judging her, thinking she was awkward and aimless and rude. But she just couldn't sit there another minute listening to their talk about computerized animation or advertising logos.

She quickly crossed the room, making her way between small groups of people. Snippets of conversation floated toward her as she passed.

"My father's stockbroker—"

"I told my analyst that I couldn't face another summer in France—"

"We fired him. He was so unreliable—"

Olivia kept her head down. *These people are so different from me*, she thought as she hurried past. *They have everything planned: goals targeted, income figured, career strategies programmed* . . .

And she had only a ridiculous dream about being an "artist." She didn't even know what that meant anymore. Maybe lots of artists did end up working in advertising or becoming architects. No one could make a living as a painter. Imagining that she could was the height of recklessness.

Ahead of her was a set of sliding glass doors leading to a deck. Olivia slipped outside, away from the busy, immaculate crowd, and stood leaning against the railing. The sun was almost gone, but vivid bands of red and violet stretched across the horizon. Olivia drew several deep breaths while she watched the play of colors. Waves crashed down below on the beach.

Then Olivia looked up and down the long, broad deck. A hot tub occupied one end of it, and elegant teak chairs with canvas cushions were scattered around. She knew it cost plenty of money to have access to sunsets in these lavish surroundings. But it must be wonderful to be able to enjoy this pleasure every single evening.

Suddenly, Olivia imagined James's fire escape. His "deck," as he called it, his reality, could not be more different than the reality of *this* deck, overlooking the ocean.

Do I want to live on processed cheese and be forced to look at the backs of other buildings all my life? Olivia demanded of herself angrily.

No, she thought. *I do not.*

Fifteen

On Sunday morning, Olivia sat down to read through the newspaper. She paid special attention to the business section and puzzled through news items about corporate takeovers and stockholders meetings. She couldn't follow most of what she read, but she assumed that it only took some practice before she became familiar with the information.

"Emily," Olivia said a little later, when they were both making their beds, "do you mind if I take a look at some of your college brochures?"

Her cousin looked at her with an expression of pleasant surprise. "Really?"

"Really. I thought I should start getting a feel for the different kinds of colleges," Olivia said.

"And I promise not to mess up your filing system!"

"Don't worry about that." Emily laughed and opened her briefcase. "I can always reorganize." She pulled out the stack of file folders and placed them on Olivia's desk.

"Great. Thanks a lot." Olivia sat at her desk and pulled a spiral notebook out of her pile of homework books. She wasn't exactly sure what she would need to take notes on, but she figured something would occur to her as she worked.

"Let me just tell you what the colored tabs mean," Emily offered. "The blue tabs mean it's a university that offers advanced degrees. Yellow tabs mean it's a four-year college. A red tab means that the college or university offers business and prelaw courses. Not that you're interested in business or prelaw."

Olivia nodded. "You never know," she said. "I might surprise you and end up studying finance."

"You're kidding."

"Nope," Olivia insisted. "Don't forget, Dad's in finance. Maybe I have some financial genes that are finally kicking in."

"Sounds like a virus," Emily teased.

"But seriously," Olivia went on, "I've done a lot of thinking, and it's clear to me now that if you want things to work out for you in your life, you really have to plan for them."

"It's true," Emily said. "Well, I'll leave you alone now," she added as she headed for the door.

After an hour of reading, Olivia's head was filled with facts about majors, early decision applications, SAT scores, graduate school requirements, junior year abroad programs, winter break internships, and financial packages from over a dozen colleges and universities. Her head was swimming, but she told herself that at least she was starting to get a sense of what was ahead of her.

She opened her spiral notebook to a fresh page and chewed on the end of her pencil. Then she wrote some headings across the top of the page: "Career Options," "Best Major for That Field," and "Best School for That Major."

Then she chewed on her pencil again while she thought some more. Practical career choices did not immediately pop into her head, but finally she thought of "art gallery owner." She wrote it down, and under the next heading she wrote "business."

Olivia felt very pleased with herself. There must be dozens of other careers in the arts that didn't carry the uncertainty and riskiness of being a painter, Olivia thought.

"This makes a lot of sense," she said out loud.

She stretched her arms and hung her head over the back of her chair. Then she stood up and took stock of herself in the mirror. It was time for all those arty clothes to move to the back of her closet, she decided, and time to get some more tailored things. On Monday at work she could ask Robert for more advice about buying the right kind of clothes to go with her new image.

"And this hair," she added, pulling her wild mop up into a ponytail and letting it flop down onto her shoulders again. She swung her head back and forth. Such long, unruly hair was totally impractical. It took forever to brush, and unless she put it up, it wisped out all over the place. How could she expect to be taken seriously if she looked like a Grateful Dead groupie?

Olivia picked up a pair of scissors and marched into the bathroom. She stared at her reflection again, then grabbed a lock of hair and snipped it off. As she looked at the hair in her hand, she was overcome with regret. For as long as she could remember, she had had long hair. It was her trademark.

"But not anymore," she said firmly.

She snipped off another handful of hair. Her curls sprang up to frame her face. It was the right thing to do, Olivia kept telling herself as she cut. She was becoming a whole new person.

"Olivia?" came her mother's voice from the hallway.

Olivia turned guiltily toward the open door. "Um, I'll be right out, Mom," she said.

And then Mrs. Davidson appeared in the doorway. Her eyes opened wide with alarm.

"*Olivia*. What have you done?" she gasped.

Olivia raised her chin. "I just decided to cut my hair," she announced defiantly.

"Oh, but honey." Mrs. Davidson bit her lip. "What made you want to do that?"

"Because it made me look like a hippie," Olivia said, turning back to the mirror. She patted her bobbed hair with an expression of satisfaction that was partly for her mother's benefit and partly to reassure herself that she hadn't made a mistake.

Mrs. Davidson shook her head. "Liv, it was the perfect look for you."

"Not anymore," Olivia said. "Besides, Mom, you were always trying to get me to do something with it."

"Well, I know, but—" Mrs. Davidson shook her head again. "I didn't think you'd do something so drastic."

Olivia shrugged.

"Olivia, is everything OK?" her mother asked suddenly. "You've seemed very moody, very deep in thought lately."

"I have been deep in thought," Olivia agreed slowly. "I just think it's time . . ." She didn't know how to finish.

Mrs. Davidson was silent for a moment. Then she picked up a hairbrush and began to brush Olivia's hair. "How's your painting going?" she asked.

"All right, I guess," Olivia replied. "I haven't had very much time for it lately. You know, with working at the store and everything."

Olivia met her mother's troubled gaze in the mirror. Mrs. Davidson opened her mouth to speak, but Olivia shook her head. "Don't worry about it, Mom. I'm doing what I want to do."

"You're sure?" Mrs. Davidson asked.

Olivia paused. "Yes." Olivia kissed her mother on the cheek. "Positive."

When she went to school the next day, Olivia was greeted by a lot of startled looks. Lila and Jessica stopped in their tracks and did a double take. Olivia smiled. She certainly had surprised people by changing her image. And she had no doubt that everyone approved of the change, too. Well, almost everyone.

"Olivia, what did you do?" Elizabeth cried in a horrified voice when they met outside their English class. She reached out to touch Olivia's hair.

"I cut it," Olivia said with a twinge of impatience.

Elizabeth shook her head. "But I loved your hair long. It was so beautiful and exotic."

"Well, it wasn't very professional-looking," Olivia explained tersely.

"Professional?" Elizabeth asked.

Olivia nodded and walked to her desk. "Right. I'm not living in the sixties, Liz."

Elizabeth's cheeks were pink. "Oh . . . So, how's your painting class going, anyway?"

"I'm dropping it," Olivia told her.

"Dropping it?" Elizabeth repeated blankly.

Olivia looked away from her friend. "Right. It just isn't—it's not what I want anymore."

"But Liv," Elizabeth protested, her face full of disappointment.

Mr. Collins, their English teacher, walked into the room and stopped suddenly. "Olivia Davidson?" His eyes opened wide. "Is that you?"

"Yes, it's me!" Olivia retorted in exasperation. "You'd think I'd committed some kind of crime," she muttered.

Olivia was angry. Everyone seemed to assume that she had made some kind of crazy, irrational decision, but she *hadn't*. It was a change for the better, and it was a *real* change. She had thought it all through: her hair, her clothes, her painting. If her friends thought she was just going to drift along in life, dabbling with paint and strumming her guitar, then they would just have to think again.

She got out her notebook and consulted the list she had written down: ask guidance office for college brochures; clean postcards and clippings out of locker; check out careers section in library.

Olivia flipped the notebook over and saw a sketch she had drawn on the back cover. It was a simple line drawing of her left hand. Looking at it gave her a strange, painful feeling. With a frown, she scribbled over and over it until it was obliterated.

"Are you working today at Simpson's?" Elizabeth asked quietly. "I can give you a ride."

"Thanks, but I have to go home first," Olivia said.

"Do you want to talk about it?" Elizabeth asked suddenly.

"Talk about going home first?" Olivia asked brightly, deliberately misunderstanding her friend. "Listen, I'll see you at the store."

Luckily, Mr. Collins started the class just then. Olivia knew that Elizabeth was too conscientious a student to talk during class. And she was too polite to push Olivia into talking if Olivia didn't want to. That was good, Olivia thought. Because she *didn't* want to talk about what she was doing. She was just doing it.

After school, Olivia took the bus home. Emily was out visiting another college, and Mrs. Davidson was at work. Olivia hurried upstairs to change and stood looking into her closet. Already she had worn her most conservative outfits to Simpson's, and she didn't have anything else that wasn't ridiculously juvenile and arty.

Hanging next to one of her sundresses was Emily's navy-blue suit. Olivia bit her lip thoughtfully as she pulled it from the closet and held it up against her. Olivia nodded and then changed into the suit.

She slid a matching navy-blue headband into her hair and adjusted the cuffs of the plain white blouse she had put on underneath the jacket. "Perfect," she said.

Robert was standing behind a counter with his back to her. Olivia smoothed her jacket and cleared her throat.

Robert turned around with a polite smile. Then he opened his eyes wide. "Olivia! You look—you look great."

Olivia grinned. "A little different, huh?"

"Sure, but it's terrific," he said, beaming. "I like your hair that way."

"Do you?" Olivia shook her head to make her curls jiggle. It still felt strange not to have the weight of her hair on her shoulders. But she could tell from the look in Robert's eyes that he approved of the change in her.

She knew she was becoming much more the kind of girl he liked to be with, and she appreciated that. It meant that she was becoming more adult, more in charge of her life.

"I'm thinking of getting some more new clothes today," she told him. "Do you have any suggestions?"

"You know, we have a personal shopper service here," he teased.

"I'd rather let you help me," she replied playfully.

"No problem. Hey, I have some great news for you, too," he went on eagerly. "I told my father about your painting—you know, the picture of the beach that I liked so much?"

Olivia nodded. "Does he want to buy it?" she joked.

"Even better," Robert said. "He says if I'm really sure your work is good, which it is, we can try putting some of your paintings in the decorating department and see if they sell."

"Are you serious?"

"I'm very serious," Robert went on. "There's a good market for pictures like that. And for your still lifes, too. I bet they'll go like that." Robert snapped his fingers.

"Wow," Olivia said. "That's amazing."

She could hardly believe her ears. *Her* paintings would be for sale in Simpson's department store! It only proved that the changes she had been making lately were *smart* changes.

Everything is falling into place, Olivia realized. And all it had taken was a new perspective on her life, a new approach. She knew for sure now that she was doing the right thing.

Sixteen

Olivia was trying on one of her two new skirts after dinner on Friday evening when the phone rang.

"For you, Olivia!" Mr. Davidson called.

She went out into the hall to pick up the extension. "Hello?"

"It's James. How are you?"

Olivia felt a stab of guilt. She had hardly thought about James recently. He was still her friend, but she hadn't once considered how he fit into her new pattern.

"Hi," she said uncomfortably. "What's new?"

"I was hoping we could get together before the holiday crunch," James said cheerfully. "Maybe we could finally see that Buñuel movie tomorrow night. Do you still want to?"

"Oh. Oh, sure," Olivia replied.

"You haven't been sick, have you?" James asked. "Is that why you weren't in class this week?"

A flaming blush swept across Olivia's cheeks. She couldn't bring herself to tell him she was dropping the class. *He would never understand*, she thought.

"No, I'm not sick," she said. "I've just been really busy. You know, school and Christmas shopping and everything. . . ."

"Sure, I know how it is," James replied. "That's why I want to make sure we can get together."

"That would be nice," Olivia replied.

For a moment, Olivia considered telling James about the paintings she was going to display at Simpson's. But something held her back. She knew how strongly James felt about the purity of art, about art for art's sake. He probably didn't care if he ever sold a painting as long as he could continue to create the kind of paintings he wanted to create.

"So, do you want to meet outside the movie theater?" Olivia asked instead.

"Sure, or you could come here to my place and I could send out for pizza," James offered.

Olivia hesitated. She wasn't sure she wanted to go to James's depressing apartment again. It would be too much of a reminder of things that were in the past now. But then she changed her mind. She was secure in the decision she had made. Going to James's place wouldn't affect her in any way. Seeing James wouldn't make her feel anything.

"Sure," she agreed. "The movie starts at eight, so why don't I come over around six?"

"Good. It'll be great to see you, Olivia. We can have one of our intense talks. Bye." James hung up abruptly.

Olivia wandered back to her room and absent-mindedly pulled the price tag off the second of her new skirts. She brooded over James's words. He thought of her as someone he could really talk to. But she wasn't sure she *could* talk to him anymore.

Open on the bed was a brochure from a small New England college. The page showed three college girls in corduroy pants and Shetland sweaters walking arm in arm through colorful autumn leaves. Olivia stared at the picture. Everything about the girls conveyed respectability, tradition, stability, security. That was the kind of life Olivia wanted. And that was what she was going to have.

Friday afternoon, Jessica went into the employees' lounge on her break. Robert was there by himself, seated at a round table, drinking a cup of coffee and studying some inventory lists.

"Hi," Jessica said cheerfully. "It's Robert, right? I'm Jessica, remember me?"

"Sure," he said with a friendly smile. "Infants and children."

Jessica got herself a can of diet soda from the machine and sat down across from him. "That's me. It sure gets crazy around this time of year, doesn't it? Say," she added, as though the idea had just come into her mind, "you know Lila Fowler, right?"

"Lila? Yes, I've seen her at country club dances," Robert agreed.

"Well, she's my very best friend," Jessica explained. "She's having a little party tonight, sort of a holiday party. Why don't you come? I bet she would be glad to have you."

The person who would be glad to have you is me! Jessica thought. And if Robert chose to look deep into her eyes, he would see her meaning.

But Robert just shook his head. "Sorry, I'd like to, but I've got other plans tonight."

"Don't tell me you have a girlfriend," Jessica said dramatically.

He smiled. "I'm going out with another friend of yours. Olivia Davidson."

"Olivia?" Jessica gulped, trying not to let her surprise show. "Gee, I would never have guessed you two were friends. She's . . . you know."

"She's what?" he asked.

Jessica waved her hand in an airy gesture.

"She's sort of the coffeehouse type. You know, folk music festivals, craft fairs, art shows, all that stuff."

Robert looked surprised. "Well, not really. I mean, she's artistic, but she's not *that* type of artistic."

"Hmm." Jessica smiled and sipped her soda. True, Olivia had undergone some kind of miraculous metamorphosis lately. In fact, she was beginning to look much more normal, more like everyone else at Sweet Valley High. But secretly, Jessica doubted that Olivia had changed all that much. Or if she had changed, it was only a temporary thing.

She stood up. "Well, I'll see you around the store, I guess."

"Sure. Bye, Jessica," Robert said.

Jessica strolled out of the lounge.

Robert seemed very interested in the new Olivia. But Jessica was sure Olivia would revert back to her old self, the old Olivia that someone like Robert wouldn't look at twice.

And when that happened, Jessica would be there waiting for him.

Olivia looked down at the menu in front of her. *Medallions of veal in a delicate tarragon marinade, served with browned new potatoes and steamed baby vegetables.*

Then she looked around the restaurant.

Gleaming crystal and silver, crisp white linen tablecloths, tuxedoed waiters. The restaurant was the height of elegance and sophistication. Finally, her eyes settled on Robert, sitting across the table from her.

". . . of the market analysis," he was saying as he perused the menu. "So San Diego looks good."

Olivia frowned. She had lost track of the conversation for a moment, and she wasn't really sure what he was talking about. She nodded with feigned interest.

Robert glanced up at her with a smile. "You look really nice tonight," he said. "Didn't I tell you that green dress was perfect for you?"

"Thanks," Olivia replied, blushing. "I have to admit, I never would have picked it out for myself, but you . . ."

"I knew it was you," he insisted.

Suddenly, Olivia found herself thinking of the musical *My Fair Lady*. Just like Professor Henry Higgins transformed Eliza Doolittle, Robert was transforming her into a sophisticated and worldly person.

At least I don't need elocution lessons, she told herself with a giggle.

"What's so funny?" Robert asked.

"Nothing," Olivia replied.

"Do you know what you want to order yet?" he asked.

Olivia looked down at the menu again.

"Oh, sorry." Everything on it sounded so elaborate that she just couldn't make up her mind. She wished they had gone to a Chinese restaurant, or that they had just ordered a pizza. She would feel a lot more comfortable and relaxed.

For a moment, Olivia wondered how James would react to a place like this. Would he even notice how glamorous and luxurious it was? Or would he put his elbows on the table and sketch on the linen napkins?

". . . I always knew that I would," Robert was saying.

Olivia pulled herself up with a snap. She felt guilty for thinking of James when she was with Robert. And she also felt guilty for not paying attention to what Robert was saying. He was probably still talking about his family's plans to expand the business to other parts of California.

"I'll have the green salad and the roast chicken," Olivia announced. It was the least expensive item on the menu. Still, the price was pretty shocking. James could probably stretch that much money over two weeks. A few cans of soup, some boxes of cereal—

Olivia's thoughts came to a screeching halt. She was thinking about James again, and it bothered her.

"So, do you think you'll get a business degree?" Olivia asked Robert politely.

"That's what I said. An MBA," Robert answered.

"Oh, right," Olivia said quickly, realizing she hadn't heard him the first time. "I meant, an undergraduate business degree, too."

"Well, I've thought about that," Robert said. "It might be better to major in economics."

"Mmm." Olivia sipped her water, and her eyes wandered around the restaurant again. With an effort, she pulled herself back to listen to Robert. He wasn't boring. It was just that she didn't really understand a lot of the things he talked about. It wasn't *his* fault that he couldn't keep her attention for more than three minutes at a time.

For the rest of the meal, Olivia forced herself to listen to Robert and to contribute sensible comments to the conversation. By the time dinner was over, she was exhausted.

"Do you want to see a movie?" Robert asked as they headed out to the parking lot.

"Oh, I don't think so," Olivia said hesitantly. "I'm actually pretty tired."

Robert nodded. "It's been a long day. I'll drive you home."

"Thanks."

About half an hour later, Olivia waved good-bye from the front porch as Robert drove away. Then she walked inside, closed the door, and leaned against it wearily.

"Olivia? Is that you?" her mother asked,

174

coming into the hall. "Hi, sweetie. Did you have a good time with Robert?"

"Mmm," Olivia said.

"So? Can't you tell me a little bit about it?" her mother asked.

Olivia looked up at the ceiling for inspiration. "The restaurant was really nice. You and Dad should go there sometime. The service was great."

"That's nice," her mother said with an encouraging smile. "What else?"

"Oh, well, I had a green salad that was really good, and roast chicken. And chocolate cake for dessert," Olivia added.

"And Robert?" Mrs. Davidson pressed.

Olivia sighed. "He had swordfish."

"Honey, I don't mean that. I mean, did you have a good time with Robert?" Mrs. Davidson said. "I've heard all about the service and the food, but you haven't said anything about what a nice time you had with Robert."

"Oh." Olivia smiled. "I had a really nice time with Robert. It was a lot of fun," she insisted.

Mrs. Davidson arched her eyebrows skeptically. "You don't sound very convincing," she said.

Olivia let out a surprised laugh. "Sorry. I didn't mean to sound that way. I had a terrific time. *Really*."

"Well, I'm glad, honey," Mrs. Davidson said doubtfully. She headed for the living room.

"Don't forget to hang up that dress. Velvet wrinkles easily and it's hard to iron."

Olivia nodded and waved cheerfully at her mother, but inside she felt empty and angry. *Why didn't she believe me when I said I had fun with Robert?* she asked herself.

She shook her head irritably. *What is wrong with me?* she wondered. *I had a great time tonight.*

But when Olivia took off her dress, she had an impulse to wad it into a ball and throw it into the back of her closet.

Instead, she hung it up carefully.

Seventeen

Elizabeth decided to go for a bike ride on Saturday afternoon. The sun was bright in a clear blue sky, and a warm ocean breeze scented the air with salt. Elizabeth rode down the street, admiring the Christmas decorations on the houses.

Sometimes she wished that there could be snow in Sweet Valley at Christmastime. It seemed funny to have colored lights in palm trees and to see plastic Santa Claus sleighs complete with reindeer on the roofs of Spanish-style houses. But Elizabeth loved California, even if it didn't look like a winter wonderland. And besides, it didn't take snow and sleigh bells and sparkling icicles to make Christmas a magical time of year.

As she turned down Olivia's street, Elizabeth thought about how Olivia had changed recently. It gave her a sad feeling to see her friend looking and acting so differently. She knew there was no reason *not* to make some alterations in one's lifestyle. But the alterations Olivia had made didn't seem sincere somehow. They just didn't seem natural to *Olivia*.

Elizabeth headed for the Davidsons' house and pulled up in the driveway. The garage door was open. Inside the garage, Olivia was standing in front of her easel, absorbed in work.

"Liv!" Elizabeth called out. "You're painting!"

Olivia looked around in surprise. She was dressed in gym shorts and a polo shirt. "Oh, hi, Liz."

"I was just riding around," Elizabeth explained as she propped her bicycle against the wall. "I thought I'd drop in and see what's new."

She smiled and walked over to look at the painting on the easel. It was a still life of fruit, painted with careful precision. Elizabeth felt a sinking sensation in her stomach.

"What's this?" she asked, trying to keep her voice casual.

Olivia scratched her cheek with the end of her paintbrush. "It's for Simpson's," she said, picking up another dab of paint from her palette. "Robert's father agreed to put some of my work in the decorating department. He's sure they'll sell. People like this kind of thing. You even said you do, remember?"

"Oh. That's right, I guess I did." Elizabeth glanced covertly at her friend, and then back at the painting.

Olivia sighed.

"What's wrong?" Elizabeth asked softly.

"Wrong?" Olivia asked. "Nothing's wrong."

Elizabeth dug her hands into her pockets. "I thought you seemed sort of depressed, that's all."

"No way," Olivia said with a bright laugh. "I'm really excited about having my pictures for sale at Simpson's."

Elizabeth nodded and looked away. "Where are your abstract paintings?" she asked. "I don't see them around."

"I put them away," Olivia replied abruptly.

Elizabeth turned back and stared at her friend. Olivia kept her eyes steadily on the canvas in front of her.

"Well," Elizabeth said uncomfortably, "I guess I should get going."

Olivia smiled at her. "Thanks for stopping by."

Reluctantly, Elizabeth began to walk away. She stopped once and looked back at Olivia. Her friend was halfheartedly adding highlights to the painted fruit. Then Elizabeth got back on her bicycle and rode away.

*   *   *

When Elizabeth had gone, Olivia put her paintbrush down and stared moodily at her painting. It was just the sort of picture that Robert liked, the sort of picture that most people liked. But at the moment, she didn't feel like working on it anymore.

Olivia turned her back on the painting and began to clean her brushes and palette. She could easily finish it the next day. Now, she would get ready to go over to James's apartment for dinner.

Olivia went to her room and put on her new pleated wool skirt, a turtleneck, and a cardigan sweater. The traditional, tailored clothes were reassuring to her. They were further symbols of the decision she had made. They represented solidity and security, a future without risks.

She walked to her desk and opened a little box that sat on top. Inside was a brass paperweight in the shape of the letter *J*. She had found it in the menswear department, in the executive-gifts section. It had a wonderfully solid, substantial feeling to it. Olivia was sure James would appreciate having something of quality. It was his Christmas gift.

When she was ready to go, Olivia asked her father for the car keys and drove over to James's place. She parked by the curb and sat looking out at the street. An empty Styrofoam cup blew into the gutter while she watched. A homeless woman was pushing a loaded shopping cart down the sidewalk. Olivia shuddered. It was depressing, dirty, and hopeless.

The familiar dark stairway echoed with her footsteps as she climbed. Almost without thinking, Olivia hugged her arms around herself, as though to keep from touching anything. She was right to reject this kind of life, she told herself firmly. Absolutely right.

"Olivia?" James opened the door at the top of the stairs and stood in silhouette. "I heard you coming up."

She smiled and climbed the last few steps. When she entered the circle of light in the doorway, James noticed her outfit and her hair. His eyes widened slightly but he didn't say anything.

"How are you?" Olivia asked as she walked ahead of him into the apartment.

"Great," James said, shutting the door.

He looked the way he always looked. His faded jeans were streaked with paint, and he was wearing an old blue T-shirt with a hole in one shoulder.

"Are you working?" Olivia asked, nodding toward the easel. She did not approach it.

James rubbed his hands together eagerly and crossed the room. "Yes, like a crazy man. If I can get this next painting finished before

Christmas, the gallery will give me an advance. And I could sure use it," he added with a smile. "I'd be able to pay the rent."

"That would be helpful," Olivia said with some of her old wryness. She looked around for something to sit on that wouldn't mess up her new clothes. She settled for a rickety chair on which sat a clean copy of the morning paper.

"So," James said, hitching himself up onto the window sill. He looked at her with an open, expectant expression. "What's new?"

"Not much," Olivia said evasively. "Let's order our pizza."

James shrugged and picked the phone up off the floor. "What do you like on it? Sausage and mushrooms OK?"

"Fine," Olivia agreed.

Olivia felt suddenly restless. She stood up and began to pace. Everywhere she looked she saw evidence of the poverty that constituted James's life. A cracked mug with no handle was draining by the sink. She picked it up while he called in their pizza order.

"How do you hold this?" she asked in a mock scolding tone. "Why don't you get one with a handle?"

James shrugged, still on the phone. "It works. If it's too hot to hold, I let it cool off."

Olivia put the mug down. She felt dumb for having made such a comment. She continued to wander. The contrast between James's apartment and the house owned by Robert's friend was enormous. *The contrast between us is enormous*, Olivia thought. James was slaving away to finish one painting so that he could pay his rent. With hardly any effort, she would sell one of her still lifes at Simpson's.

I'll never have to go through this kind of grind, she told herself with a trace of smugness. Then she overheard James saying "thank you" in his comfortable, uncomplaining way, and she felt very small inside.

"So tell me," James said when he had hung up the phone. "Did you just come from a board of trustees meeting or something?"

"What do you mean?" Olivia asked.

He extended one paint-encrusted finger and pointed to her clothes. "When you walked in here, I thought at first you were the lady who tried to sell me life insurance last week."

"So I'm wearing nice clothes," Olivia said huffily. "What's the big deal?"

"No big deal. I just thought it was some kind of a joke, that's all." James laughed.

Olivia's face flamed red. "I'm not trying to make a joke," she informed him. "If you want to know the truth, the way I *used* to dress was a joke."

"What? The way you used to dress was the *truth*, Olivia."

"Oh, come on." Olivia flung her arms up and

183

let them drop by her side. "That whole artistic look was just an act, just a costume. I don't need that anymore."

Laughing, James stood up and began to clear off the table. "Why? Are you going to tell me you've joined the world of free trade and commerce or something? That you don't need art anymore?"

"Well, now that you mention it, I guess I have," Olivia said. "I've done a lot of thinking lately and I've decided to start planning for my future, to start thinking about a career. And," she added before he could cut in, "I haven't given up art. As a matter of fact, some of my paintings are on display at Simpson's department store."

James turned and looked carefully at her. "In a *department* store?" he asked.

"Yes." Olivia felt another wave of embarrassment and confusion wash over her.

"I can't see your paintings in a department store." James laughed again and shook his head.

"Not my abstracts," Olivia said quickly. "I've done some really nice still lifes. I'm not wasting my time on abstracts any longer. There's no future in them."

James sat down at the table and rested his chin in his hand. He stared at her silently, and Olivia returned his stare for as long as she could. The silence stretched out so long that she wanted to scream.

"I can't believe you just said that," James said at last. "Future? Wasting time? How can you say that, Olivia? How can you *say* that?"

"Easily. I just did." Olivia turned away. She knew she sounded childish, but she couldn't help it. James was making her feel all defensive and stuffy.

"Are you the same person I used to talk to?" James asked. "Are you the same person who agreed that painting is something you *have* to do, something that's part of who you are?"

"That was before," Olivia said irritably. She began to pace again, and made nervous gestures with her hands as she continued. "I'm not going to spend my life starving for some kind of ideal. I like having nice clothes and living in a nice house. I don't want to live in a place like *this*."

Olivia could feel James's eyes on her, and she prickled with indignation and confusion. He was making her say things she didn't really mean! He was making her sound cold and materialistic and rude. He was making her defend positions she suddenly wasn't really sure she wanted to defend!

"Look, I'm sorry I just said that," she said quickly. "I didn't mean to insult you."

James shrugged one shoulder. "I'm not insulted. I know I live in a slum."

"And you don't care," Olivia countered.

"And I don't care," he repeated. He gestured

toward the paintings propped against the walls. "This is all I care about, Olivia. I thought you felt the same way about your work."

Olivia swallowed hard over the lump in her throat.

"Well, I used to," she admitted finally. "But don't you see, I'm trying to plan ahead. I *would* care if I ended up living in a slum. Maybe that's really shallow, but I can't help it."

"Yes, you can." James spoke simply.

Her mind whirling, Olivia strode to the window and stared out at the darkness. She had to get her focus back, get centered again on her decision. James was trying to confuse her. She was sure she could summon back her sense of security if only she could think for a moment, if only she could collect her thoughts. If only she could ignore the way he made her feel inside.

Olivia took a deep breath to steady herself. "Look, I don't want to fight about this," she said. She looked at James over her shoulder. "I brought you a Christmas present. Let me give it to you now."

Before he could say anything, Olivia ran to get her shoulder bag. She pulled out the small, heavy box and handed it to him abruptly.

"Go ahead and open it," she said coaxingly.

James smiled. "OK. Thanks." He pulled off the bow and took the lid off the box. When he parted the tissue paper, the smile froze on his face.

"It's a paperweight," Olivia said.

"I can see it's a paperweight," James replied. He put the lid back on and handed her the box.

Olivia's stomach flip-flopped. "What?"

"I don't want it," James said bluntly. "I don't want a gift like this from you, Olivia."

Hurt and embarrassed, Olivia shoved the box back at him. "It was very expensive, you know," she blustered. "It's very nice."

"I don't care how much it cost," James replied. "This is the emptiest, most meaningless present anyone ever gave me."

Olivia backed up, shaking her head. She was so stunned by his reaction that she could hardly speak. "I don't understand why you don't like it."

"Gifts are supposed to reflect something about the giver," James said bitterly. "And that," he added, jabbing a finger at the paperweight, "doesn't reflect very well on you."

With tears of anger and indignation in her eyes, Olivia stuffed the box back into her shoulder bag and headed for the door.

"I should have known you wouldn't appreciate something really nice," she said hoarsely.

"Olivia." James's voice was filled with sadness.

Olivia kept her back to him. "What?" she said.

"I thought you were an artist."

"Why did I even bother?" Olivia cried, spinning around now to glare at him. "There's more to life than art and pure expression and all that stuff, you know. You won't listen to anything that isn't the Truth with a capital *T*."

"You're right. I won't," James replied.

So many emotions were raging inside her that Olivia thought she would be sick. And one of the strongest of those emotions was jealousy. She knew she had failed in an important way: She could not have faith in her own artistic vision, and James could. She envied him that.

"I can't talk to you," she said bleakly.

"How could you change like this?" he answered.

Olivia grabbed the doorknob and yanked open the door. The pizza delivery man was standing on the other side, just raising his hand to knock.

"Uh, pizza for James Yates?" the man asked, holding out the steaming box.

"That's him," Olivia said, pushing past. "He's eating alone."

Eighteen

Olivia went down to breakfast on Sunday morning, poured herself a cup of coffee, and sat at the table, pushing aside the newspaper dejectedly. Just a week ago she had confidently studied the business section. Now she didn't even feel up to reading the comics.

It had hit her that morning, while she lay staring at the ceiling over her bed. She knew she was in love with James. But she also knew—or thought she knew—that she could never live up to his standards. There was no future in it, anyway. From the very beginning James had made it plain that he was not interested in a romantic relationship. And after what had happened the night before, Olivia didn't even think they could ever be friends again.

It was better and safer for her to put her hopes in someone like Robert, in the sort of life he personified. Robert was easy to get along with, and he didn't demand that Olivia live up to ideals that frightened her—to ideals she used to share with James. No, in Robert's world it was OK to be contented. No one expected you to take unreasonable risks. *No one expects very much of anything*, Olivia thought.

"Hi, honey," Mrs. Davidson said, coming in from the patio. "It's a gorgeous day."

"That's nice," Olivia replied. She stared down into her coffee cup and saw the reflection of her own face. She blew on it, and the image shivered into fragments.

Her mother sat down across from her. "Did you have a nice time last night with your friend James?"

Olivia let out a sour laugh. "No."

"Why not?" Mrs. Davidson asked. "I thought you always had so much to talk about with him."

"Not last night." Olivia sighed. "It was a total disaster. He doesn't see things that matter in the real world. All he ever talks about is art and painting and all that high-standards stuff," Olivia blurted out.

Mrs. Davidson frowned. "But Olivia, it wasn't so long ago that that was all *you* ever talked about, too."

"Well, I don't anymore," Olivia said. "There

are other things in life. Like planning ahead, making sure all the pieces fall into place."

"Olivia, I don't understand," her mother said softly. "What's gotten into you? All this talk about careers and plans isn't like you."

Olivia shrugged and looked out the window. "It's like me now."

"But what about your painting?" Mrs. Davidson asked anxiously. "I've noticed that none of your abstracts are out in your studio."

Olivia stood up to stand at the window. She felt dull and heavy inside. "They just seem like a waste of time now."

"A waste of *time*?"

Olivia winced when she heard the shocked tone in her mother's voice. She didn't turn around.

"Olivia, painting is what you love to do," Mrs. Davidson went on. "How can you say it's a waste of time?"

"Well, the paintings that *sell* aren't a waste of time," Olivia pointed out stubbornly. "The other things—that kind of stuff just doesn't matter."

"Do you really believe that art doesn't matter?" Mrs. Davidson asked.

"Mom!" Olivia sat down again next to her mother. "I thought you *wanted* me to start thinking about my future and plan ahead for a career and all of that. I thought you wanted me to be just like Emily."

"Of course I want you to think about your future," Mrs. Davidson said. "But I didn't ask you to turn into a clone of your cousin. You two are very different people."

Olivia raised her chin stubbornly. "Maybe we're *not* so different. Maybe I think it's time to start being practical. I don't see what you're so upset about."

Mrs. Davidson's cheeks were tinged with pink. "I'm upset that you're throwing away something so wonderful."

"All I'm throwing away is life on the edge," Olivia retorted, vividly remembering James's squalid apartment. "I'm not going to kid myself that dabbling with oil paints is going to make my future all rosy and fine."

Her mother's mouth set in a line of determination. "Olivia, I want to show you something," she said.

Olivia felt a strong desire to say "No." Whatever her mother was going to show her would not take away the confusion and anxiety she was feeling. But instead, she said, "What?"

Mrs. Davidson took Olivia's hand and led her out of the kitchen in silence. Olivia followed along without protesting. She didn't have the energy to put up a fight. She didn't know what she felt or thought anymore, she didn't care what her mother was going to say to her or show her. But her curiosity was aroused when her mother led the way up to the attic.

"What, Mom?" she asked again. "What is it?" She hung back near the door, vaguely afraid of joining her mother by the stack of suitcases and cartons of old magazines.

"I want you to take a look at these," Mrs. Davidson said. She opened a cardboard box that she had pulled from underneath an old, rolled-up rug.

Mrs. Davidson reached inside and took out a brown cardboard portfolio. She untied the ribbons that held it closed, and then stood back.

Olivia walked over to her mother and knelt down to take a look. In the portfolio was a collection of small, unframed watercolor paintings.

"It's too dark," she murmured, standing up again and carrying the paintings to the window.

She held them toward the morning light. The pictures were of flowers and grasses, miniature scenes of stream banks and twigs of blossoming trees. The colors were delicate, and each picture seemed to breathe with life and light. Olivia looked at each one with a fresh sense of amazement. They were lovely.

"Where did these come from?" she asked quietly. "They're so pretty. They're really very good."

Mrs. Davidson joined Olivia by the window. "You'll never guess," she said softly.

"Tell me." Olivia looked at her mother's face, and a strange feeling stole over her. "Mom, you didn't—"

"Yes, I did," Mrs. Davidson said.

Olivia was speechless. It was inconceivable that her mother could have done anything so exquisite, so sensitive, so *artistic*.

"I did these when I was a little older than you are now," Mrs. Davidson explained wistfully. "I painted a lot when I was young."

"But what happened?" Olivia gasped. "Why did you stop?"

Her mother smiled. "I decided I'd have a career in business, and that I wouldn't have time for this sort of thing anymore. I didn't really think I had enough talent to make something of my painting, anyway. And then your father and I got married, and we had you, and my painting just got pushed further and further into the past."

"Mom," Olivia said, the tears threatening to flow.

"I'm not sorry," Mrs. Davidson said gently. She lifted Olivia's chin and looked lovingly into her eyes. "Having you and bringing you up has been more rewarding than painting the ceiling of the Sistine Chapel." Mrs. Davidson smiled. "I'm very proud of you, Olivia. I hope you realize that."

Olivia sniffed and lowered her eyes.

"Honey, there have been times I've wished

you were more practical or that you thought more about everyday things," Mrs. Davidson told her. "But then I realized that you have such a talent, such a gift. I didn't have enough of a talent to take a chance, but I think you do. Please don't just give up on it."

There was such a huge lump in Olivia's throat that she couldn't even swallow. She looked at the paintings again through her tears. To her mind, her mother *had* had a real talent for those tiny, delicate pictures. And she had given it all up, out of timidity or because of the lure of security.

Suddenly, Olivia remembered the scrap of conversation she had overheard between her mother and Aunt June. So this was what Aunt June had meant by "giving up all that foolishness." It all made sense now.

"I'm going to clean the breakfast dishes," Mrs. Davidson said, breaking the silence. "I hope you'll think about what I said."

Olivia nodded, still overcome with emotion. She listened as her mother's footsteps grew fainter, and she continued to stare almost blindly at the portfolio of watercolors.

What am I going to do? Olivia asked herself wearily.

She put the paintings back into the portfolio and tied up the ribbons again. She placed it gently back in the box. Then she went down to her room.

She saw the drawings and photographs on the walls with a strange new sense of unreality. She crossed the room to the drawing of her parents over her bed, gazed at it for a moment, and then let the tears flow.

Only a few days remained before Christmas. Emily had one more campus interview lined up, and the Davidsons had talked her into staying with them for the holiday.

"I'm glad you can stay," Olivia told her when they were in Olivia's room after dinner.

Emily looked up happily from her book. "Really?"

"Sure," Olivia said as she put away some clean clothes in her closet.

"You know, I'm pretty sure I'll be going to school out here," Emily told her. "I really like California."

Olivia nodded and hung up a skirt. "Great."

Emily observed her cousin for a few moments. It seemed to her that Olivia had been very subdued for the last couple of days. Ever since the evening Olivia had gone to see James a few days earlier, she had seemed preoccupied. Emily didn't feel close enough to Olivia to ask her what was wrong, but she did hope that Olivia would want to confide in her.

"Are you seeing Robert before Christmas?" Emily asked neutrally.

"Tomorrow afternoon," Olivia said. She closed the closet door and stood against it for a moment. "Can you give me some advice?" she asked in a hesitant voice.

Emily put her book down. "Sure. What about?"

"Well, I want to give Robert one of my paintings," Olivia said. "But lately, I feel I can't really trust my own judgment." She laughed ruefully. "You have a lot more in common with Robert than I do, so I thought you could help me pick out the one he'd like best."

"But you're the artist, not me," Emily said.

Olivia shook her head quickly. "Can't you just help me decide?" She seemed so anxious that Emily did not have the heart to refuse.

"Sure," she said. "Let's go do it now."

Together they went out to Olivia's studio. Olivia switched on the overhead light. Emily looked around curiously. Seeing James's studio, and Olivia's, had given her a glimpse of the artist's life that she found very intriguing.

"I can't decide among these three," Olivia said.

Emily joined Olivia at the long workbench. On it were three small paintings: a still life of a dish of figs, one of a sunset on the beach, and one of a window with potted geraniums on the sill. Emily knew enough about her cousin to realize that they were in the style that Olivia didn't very much care about. She thought it was odd that Olivia would want to give one of them to Robert. It made her wonder about Olivia's feelings for him.

"Well, I like the window," Emily said finally.

"Really? Do you think Robert would like it?" Olivia asked in a somewhat forlorn voice.

Emily felt like reaching out to hug Olivia. Her cousin seemed so sad and lost.

"Yes," she said quietly. "I'm sure he'll like it a lot."

"Thanks," Olivia said.

"Did you ever finish the picture you were working on when I first got here?" Emily asked quickly.

"Umm . . ." Olivia fussed with some brushes and rags. "Yes."

"Could I—" Emily began.

"I put it away," Olivia interrupted. She stood up briskly. "I should go wrap this."

She headed for the garage door and stopped. With a shrug, Emily switched off the light and followed her cousin.

Olivia wrapped Robert's painting in several sheets of colored tissue paper, yellow over pink over red. Usually she loved wrapping gifts, loved bringing her creativity to the choice of paper and bows. But now she worked half-heartedly. She tied the package up with a piece of gold ribbon. Briefly she considered making an origami bird for the top, then decided not to. It seemed like a waste of effort.

As she began to put away the tape and scissors, the phone rang. Olivia crossed the room to answer it.

"Hello?"

"Olivia?"

Olivia felt her heart contract. "Hi, James."

"Listen, about the other night," he began.

"I'm sorry," Olivia said, her voice threatening to break.

"Forget it," James replied, his voice warm and sincere. "I said some things I shouldn't have. I was out of line."

Olivia shook her head. Tears came so easily these days.

"I want to give you a Christmas present," James continued.

"Why?" Olivia managed to say.

"Because I want to," he replied. "Can you come over tomorrow sometime?"

She looked down at the tissue-wrapped painting in her hands. "I'm busy in the afternoon," she began.

"Come over afterward, then," James pleaded. "Whenever. It doesn't matter."

Deep down, Olivia thought it might be better not to go, not to see him. But she wanted to. She had to.

"All right," she whispered. "I'll come over when I can."

"I'll be here."

When Olivia hung up the phone, she stood staring into space. Instead of having sorted out her life in the last few weeks, she knew she had just stirred it up. Instead of creating order, she had created turmoil and confusion. She had a lot of thinking yet to do, and some real, hard decisions to make.

And she just didn't know how to make them.

Nineteen

After Olivia had left the next day to meet Robert, Emily sat on her bed, deep in thought. She was sure she would be going to college in California in the fall. And if she was going to be near Sweet Valley, she would be able to see James and keep up their friendship. *Maybe it wouldn't be a bad idea to solidify things before I go home*, she mused. After all, she always felt more confident and secure when she knew she had things lined up for the future.

With a resolute nod, Emily got up, opened the closet, and chose one of Olivia's colorful cotton skirts. She put on a pink T-shirt to match it, and then a black velvet vest. A string of wooden beads was the finishing touch.

Emily regarded herself in the mirror.

Did she fit at all in James's world? She knew that just changing clothes didn't change the person inside them. But now she was too eager to see James to pay attention to those doubts.

Emily got in the rental car and drove across town. She knew James didn't belong in such a depressing, gloomy place. She was sure that if they did have a relationship someday, she could change him. She could get him to move to a better part of town, to pay more attention to practical matters. She would help him to see that in order to get ahead, you had to make some compromises.

Emily parked the car a block away from James's apartment and ran the rest of the way.

"Hello?" she called when she had reached his door. "Anybody home?"

"Hey, you're early," she heard James say.

Footsteps sounded on the floor, and then James flung the door open with a wide smile. When he saw Emily, his smile fell. "Oh. Hi, Emily," he said. He looked beyond her down the stairway.

"How's it going?" Emily asked. Though she could not take her eyes off his face, she wished that he had shaved.

"Did you come with Olivia?" James asked, still trying to see past her.

Emily felt something twist inside her painfully. "No," she said, keeping her voice light. "She's over at Robert's house."

"Robert?" James repeated. He turned and wandered back inside his apartment.

Emily followed. "I told you about him, remember? He's been really great about her paintings—well, the still lifes. They're selling at the department store. Olivia's not doing the other kind of paintings anymore, the abstract ones."

"Oh, really?" James asked hollowly.

"Yes." Emily sat on the edge of a chair. The conversation wasn't going the way she had hoped. James seemed to be in a very strange mood.

"James, I wanted to tell you something," she said quickly.

He didn't look at her. He picked up a palette knife and idly picked at dried clumps of oil paint on the windowsill. "Mmm?" he murmured.

Emily drew a deep breath before going on. It was now or never, she realized. "I'll definitely be going to school out here next year. There's a lot about California I really like. Especially the people I've met."

He still didn't look at her. Emily's heart began pounding anxiously. She didn't want to throw herself at him, but she wanted him to know how she felt.

"James?" she said earnestly.

Finally, he looked at her, but Emily had a feeling that he didn't really see her.

"I was hoping we could be—friends," she blurted out at last. She squeezed her hands together to keep them from shaking.

James slowly focused his attention on her, and then gave her a distant smile. "That's what we already are, Emily. We're friends." The tone of his voice and the expression on his face told Emily that he had understood what she had been trying to say. And that his answer was no.

"Well, that's great," Emily said, hiding her regret and disappointment behind a smile. "You can never have too many friends, right?"

"Right." James turned back to prying up the dried paint from the window sill.

Suddenly, Emily saw everything clearly. She didn't know why she hadn't seen it before. James was in love with Olivia and he didn't even know it. He had talked himself into believing that there was no such thing as love, that he only had room in his heart for painting. But he had been wrong.

Emily sighed. There had never been a chance for her. Her borrowed clothes didn't change the fact that James and Olivia had a special bond that Emily could never share. She belonged to a very different world. Not a better one, or a worse one, but a very different one.

"I guess I'll see you sometime," she said as she stood up.

"Thanks for stopping by," James replied. "Merry Christmas."

"You, too," Emily said.

She walked to the door and looked back. James had already forgotten she was there. Smiling sadly, Emily opened the door and slipped out.

Olivia drove up to the large, traditional house overlooking Sweet Valley. It was very imposing, and it looked a little bit out of place, too. *This kind of house belongs in Virginia or Maryland, not California*, she thought.

Then the door opened and Robert walked out onto the porch. "Hey, what are you sitting in the driveway for?" he called. "Come on in."

With a smile, Olivia opened the car door and got out, carrying the wrapped painting. "Hi."

"Merry Christmas, almost," Robert said. "Come on inside."

Olivia followed him in, listening to his easy, charming stories about the family tree and their arguments about whether to have roast beef or turkey for their Christmas dinner. Olivia took note of the elegant Oriental carpet in the hallway, the Queen Anne cherry furniture. Everything was in perfect taste, perfectly respectable, and without imagination. She found herself hoping fervently to find a note of surprise or unexpectedness in the house.

"I brought you a Christmas present," she said as he led the way into the living room. A tall Christmas tree dripping with glass ornaments and gold bows occupied a big bay window. "I hope you like it."

He took it and then went over to the tree. "I've got something for you, too," he said, picking up a flat, rectangular box.

For a moment, Olivia kept her hands behind her back. Something in her was almost afraid to open Robert's gift. Something told her it would be in perfect taste, just like the house.

"Go on," he urged cheerfully when she had taken it.

"Open yours first," Olivia said. She sat down on a white upholstered wing chair. The present sat untouched in her lap.

Robert smiled boyishly. "Well, OK. Let's see," he said, closing his eyes and feeling the painting through the tissue paper. "It's not a basketball."

"No." Olivia laughed.

Robert tore the paper off and looked at the painting. "Wow. Nice."

Olivia felt a sense of deflation. *Nice.*

"It's one of mine," she told him.

"Sure, I guessed it was," Robert said. He propped it up on the mantelpiece next to two silver candlesticks. "That's the kind of thing I know you can sell. Thanks, Olivia," he said warmly. "It's very pretty."

Olivia tried to return his smile. After all, she reasoned, it had been her choice to paint a nice, pretty painting. There was no reason for her to be surprised by Robert's reaction, or to be hurt by it. But she was, both surprised and hurt.

"Now go on, open yours," Robert said.

Olivia stared down at the present that sat in her lap. "You want me to open it now?" she asked reluctantly.

"Go on!" Robert chuckled. "It's not going to bite you, you know."

"All right." Olivia carefully slid her fingers under the tape and unwrapped the present. It was a Filofax organizer, with a red leather cover. She couldn't think of a single thing to say about it.

All she could think of was what James had said about gifts, that they reflected something about the giver. Robert's choice of an expensive organizer reflected something about him that Olivia didn't really want to admit: that his image of her was that of a person who would *want* a Filofax, of a person to whom schedules and business contacts were a way of life, just as they were for him.

"I already put an entry into the address section," Robert told her. "Look under *S*."

Obediently, Olivia turned to the tab marked S and opened it up. Written in neat script was Robert's name, address, and phone number.

"Great," she said numbly.

Olivia raised her eyes to his face. His smile was so eager, so hopeful, that her heart went out to him. Robert was sweet and kind and generous. But he wasn't for her. And his life-style wasn't for her, either. It was all very clear to her now. She was glad to realize it, but sad, too. All it meant was that she still didn't know who or what she was or what she wanted out of life. She was no closer to finding Olivia Davidson than she had been weeks ago.

Olivia cleared her throat. "Thanks," she whispered as she put the Filofax down on the chair beside her. "It's really sweet of you."

"I'm glad you like it." Robert took a step closer to her and looked down into her eyes.

Olivia knew he wanted to kiss her, to seal some kind of agreement. He thought they had something that she now knew was just a mis-guided fantasy.

"I have to go," she said abruptly, standing up and moving away from him.

Robert looked startled and hurt. "You do? I thought you might be able to stay for dinner— or we could go out?"

"I can't." Olivia shook her head. "I—my fam-ily's expecting me," she lied.

"Well, if you have to go . . ." Robert said reluctantly.

"I'm sorry." Olivia started toward the door.

"Wait—you forgot your Filofax," Robert exclaimed.

Blushing, Olivia took it from him and gave him a tender smile. She wished she could feel differently about him, but she couldn't.

"I'll see you at work," she said as she headed out the door.

Robert stood on the porch, watching her walk away. Olivia kept her eyes on the car and went straight to it without looking back. There was no way to explain.

When Olivia got home, she headed up to her room. As she stood by her desk, she heard Emily's car pull up in the driveway. A few minutes later, Emily walked into Olivia's room, too.

"Oh, Olivia," Emily said awkwardly. "I didn't know you were home."

Olivia turned, and her eyes widened. Her cousin was wearing her clothes.

"I would have asked if I could borrow these," Emily said embarrassedly. "I hope you don't mind."

"No, I don't mind," Olivia said slowly.

For a moment, they stood looking at each other—Olivia wearing a khaki skirt and polo shirt, and Emily wearing Olivia's blue print skirt and black vest.

"Look at us," Emily said with a laugh. "We're dressed as each other."

"I know." Olivia shook her head and smiled.

Emily sat down on her bed. "We've both been trying to be something we're not," she said tiredly.

Olivia's heart went out to her cousin. In spite of Emily's precise, orderly, businesslike manner, there was obviously a part of her that craved a freer form of expression. Just as there was a part of Olivia that craved order and tradition. And each of them had to be true to her own real nature, no matter what. Olivia could see that now.

"That outfit looks nice on you, though," she said to her cousin.

"You don't look so bad yourself," Emily returned playfully.

Then they both laughed. "But let's trade," Olivia begged.

"OK," Emily said. She looked down at her skirt and shrugged. "I do sort of feel like I'm playing dress-up, you know."

"That's what I've been feeling lately, too." Olivia lay back on the bed. "Listen, you know that green dress I just bought?"

"The velvet one? I love it."

"You can have it," Olivia said. "Merry Christmas."

Twenty

Olivia climbed the familiar dingy stairs to James's apartment. From behind one of the other apartment doors came the sound of a radio playing Christmas music. A child shrieked excitedly and then burst into a peal of laughter. Olivia smiled. Even here, the Christmas spirit was strong. She tucked the bulky package under her arm and knocked on James's door.

When he opened it, James stood silently on the threshold. Olivia realized she was scared.

"So, Olivia," he said, breaking into a smile. His eyes traveled down to take in her long purple sweater and black leggings. Beyond him, lighted candles cast a warm glow over the paintings and old furniture.

"Hi," she replied. She felt self-conscious and

nervous, almost lightheaded. She still wasn't sure what she was going to say to him.

He stepped aside and waved her in. Olivia lowered her head shyly and went inside.

"I just made some tea," he told her. "Do you want some?"

The apartment was exactly the same as it had been the last time she was there. But for some reason, Olivia didn't see the poorness now. Instead, she saw the vitality of the canvases; she felt the spirit of truth and beauty and honesty.

James was watching her with hope in his eyes. "Olivia, I—"

"I brought you your real Christmas present," Olivia broke in. She handed him her package.

James looked at her for a moment, and then took the package to the cluttered table and cleared some space on the surface. Then he untied the ribbon and ripped off the paper. Olivia held her breath.

"This is a real present," he whispered, looking intently at the "Mother and Child" painting.

Olivia felt tears come to her eyes, and she quickly brushed them away.

James finally looked up at her, and a warm, understanding smile spread across his face. Olivia realized that, somehow, James knew that it was the best thing she had ever done, that she didn't know if she would ever be able to do anything like it again.

"Forget the tea," he said. "I want to give you your present now."

"You didn't have to," Olivia said.

"Yes, I did. But we have to go out for it," he replied, grinning excitedly. He strode toward her and grabbed her hand. "Come on."

Olivia hung back. "What? What is it? Where are we going?"

"It's a surprise," he said, pulling her toward the door. "Let's go."

A feeling of elation made Olivia's heart soar. She knew that James wouldn't be giving her a Filofax or a sensible, practical gift. She knew that whatever it was would be special, magical. She ran down the stairs behind him, laughing.

Together, they walked toward the coffee shop in the middle of the block. She was aching to know what his gift was going to be. But it was also wonderful to have some spontaneity in her life again.

"You're buying me a piece of pie?" she teased as they walked into the coffee shop.

"No questions," he said firmly, leading the way to the back door.

"It's out here?" she asked, glancing around at the garbage cans and empty crates.

"Now," James said when they stepped into the alley. "Close your eyes."

"Come on," Olivia protested.

James shook his head and put his hands across her eyes. Olivia let him lead her several

213

steps forward into the alley, and then he turned her around to face the back of the coffee shop.

"OK," he said, taking his hands away from her eyes.

Slowly, Olivia opened them. In front of her, on the brick wall, was a huge portrait of her. In fact, there were two portraits of her.

On one side of the door was a picture of Olivia with her long hair blowing around her face and feather earrings dangling from her ears. Her eyes were looking up and out. The colors were wild and exuberant, the lines splashed on the wall with abandon.

On the other side of the door was a portrait of Olivia looking straight ahead. Her hair was short and pulled neatly back, and a circular pin closed the collar at her throat. The paint was applied meticulously, carefully, and the colors were restrained.

Two Olivias. The artist and the planner, but both were Olivia.

"Which is it going to be?" James asked softly from behind her.

Olivia stared at the portraits. She thought about how she had felt while painting the "Mother and Child" picture, and about how she had forced herself to switch to the safe, conservative landscapes. Freedom or safety— she had to choose between them.

And then she remembered her mother's choice. Olivia started to tremble.

"Olivia," James whispered.

His present was the most powerful gift anyone had ever given her. It summarized the issues she had been grappling with, all of the conflicting ideas that had thrown her into an emotional whirlpool.

She had been hoping to ignore the conflict, but now she knew that it was a conflict she had to live through. Freedom with risk, or dullness with safety. She had to choose. And she had to choose now, while she was still young enough to choose well.

Olivia squeezed her eyes shut. Then she raised her hand and pointed toward the door in the middle. When it was time to go back through that door, one of the portraits was going to go with her in spirit. The other would remain behind.

With a sudden, powerful sense of fate, Olivia moved her arm and pointed to the portrait of herself as an artist. She opened her eyes. She was free. She had made her choice.

"This is me," she said. She turned to look at James.

"I knew it," he said joyfully. "That's the Olivia I love."

Olivia shook her head in disbelief. "Wh-what?"

James looked at her steadily. "When I thought you might give up painting—*really* painting—I felt as if I was losing something."

"You did?" she asked, her heart pounding.

"I thought I didn't believe in love," he told her. "But I do, Olivia. I really do."

"I'll never give up my painting, I swear," she breathed. "I don't care if I never have pearl earrings or nice clothes or a steady job. I might never make it as a painter but I'm going to try, because—"

James didn't let her finish. With a tender smile, he pulled her into his arms and kissed her. Olivia wrapped her arms around his neck. It felt right. It felt wonderful.

"Merry Christmas," he whispered in her ear. "It's great to have you back."